LANDS OF MEMORY

LANDS OF MEMORY

Felisberto Hernández

translated by ESTHER ALLEN

NEW DIRECTIONS

The two novellas and four stories contained in *Lands of Memory* (originally titled "Por los tiempos de Clemente Colling," "Tierras de memoria," "Manos equivocadas," "Il Cocodrilo," "La casa nueva," and "Mi primer concierto en Montevideo") are published by arrangement with the heirs of Felisberto Hernández, represented by Ana Maria Hernández, and with the help of Agencia Literaria Carmen Balcells.

Design by Semadar Megged
First published clothbound in 2002
Manufactured in the United States of America.

Library of Congress Cataloging-in-Publication Data:
Hernández, Felisberto.
[Selection. English. 2002]
Lands of memory / Felisberto Hernández ; translated from the Spanish by Esther Allen.
p. cm.
ISBN 0-8112-1483-4 (cloth : alk. paper)
1. Hernández, Felisberto—Translations into English. I. Allen, Esther, 1962– II. Title.
PQ8519.H34 A215   2002
863'.62—dc21   200104589

10 9 8 7 6 5

New Directions Books are published for James Laughlin
by New Directions Publishing Corporation
80 Eighth Avenue, New York 10011

TABLE OF CONTENTS

PROLOGUE: FELISBERTO

HE PUBLISHED HIS FIRST BOOK AT the age of twenty-three: it was twenty-one paragraphs long. He wrote two novels: the first 95 pages long and the second 67 pages, but he published only a fragment of the second one. During his lifetime he published ten books; their average length was 68 pages. In 1940, he started a bookstore called El burrito blanco (Little White Burro) in the garage of his second wife's family home. The store lasted only a few months because Felisberto—no one ever calls him Hernández—neglected it and instead spent his days perfecting a system of shorthand notation he had invented.

Early in his life, he noticed that art didn't matter at all to many of the people around him, and that some even found it hilarious or embarrassing. He also noticed that other people became hilarious or embarrassing in their eagerness to demonstrate their passion for art.

In 1917, at the age of fifteen, he began working at a local cinema as a "musical illustrator" of silent movies, poised between the stark geometry of the piano keyboard and the images that rippled across the screen. His family needed the money. His father was a plumber and later, briefly and disastrously, the owner of a construction company.

For the rest of his life, whenever he went to the movies, Felisberto always sat in the front row. It was the vantage point he'd grown accustomed to— "like drinking milk straight from the cow," he wrote.

An eternal child, a perennial adolescent, a hopeless provincial, a dimwit full of "inexplicable stupidities," he was the distracted student who always comes up with exactly the wrong answer, the one boy in the group who's always the last to catch on. "If all my life and my being were judged by a few incidents," he wrote, "it would rightly be determined that I was a complete imbecile."

He founded his own conservatory of music at the age of sixteen and spent twelve to sixteen hours a day practicing, and sometimes composing works of his own. His career, however, was not meteoric; he gave his first solo concert when he was twenty-four. Thirteen years later, he was hailed as a true virtuoso after a concert in Buenos Aires. Three years after that, in dire financial straits, he sold his piano and left his second wife.

He required absolute silence in order to write.

In 1944 he began working for the Uruguayan Association of Authors, in the Radio Audit section. His job was to listen to live radio broadcasts of tango music, noting down the titles of all the songs in order to ensure that the conductors paid all royalties that were due to the composers. This was ironic, he noted to a friend, for he loathed the tango. Still, he added, "all this has been a great experience for placing me more within the immediacies of life, at which I've always been so clumsy, or egotistical or idiotic." Later, one of his wives found him a job at the National Press, as a stenographer.

He was a man who cherished his illusions. He understood that knowledge inexorably accumulates and can only be forestalled for so long; it was the moments and states of mind which precede it that interested him—though his interest was fully aroused only by the strange forms those moments and states of mind took on as they came floating up out of his memory many years later when he attempted to write them down. "Writing is my last link to the present moment," he wrote. He was anywhere but here.

He had four wives and many loves besides, but he always went back to his mother. "I can't sleep in this house any longer because I'm thinking of Mama, alone in a dark room," he told his fourth wife. One of his lovers, Paulina Medeiros, a novelist herself, writes that "in a moment of marital surfeit, he left his wife's bedroom and established an endless conversation with his mother, who was a guest in their home."

He had a habit of comparing pianos to coffins, but found the piano impossible to abandon. In the last part of his life, when he hadn't played in public for many years, he continued giving piano lessons and practicing for what he told his friends would be "a big concert."

What the piano meant to him can be deduced from his description of a brief performance he gave after attending a recital at a convent school: "When I sat down at the piano and realized I was distracted, I began summoning myself with all my force, as if I were struggling to wake up from a dream. Once I'd been playing a while and was fully within myself, I looked at all the girls' faces, and their attention wasn't scattered any longer; now they were paying concrete attention to me, now they were observing the mystery that was mine."

He was struck by the importance of the spaces that separate people from each other, those spaces that create the possibility of longing, the purest and most beautiful of emotions.

Though so much of his life was dedicated to music, in his writing the eye is far more significant than the ear. His work will bring Magritte or Joseph Cornell to mind before summoning thoughts of any composer (Satie, perhaps?). But his idea of narrative is musical: he doesn't write to convince, or weave elaborate plots or contrive dazzling or devastating denouements; he neglects the ordinary mechanisms of suspense, intrigue, and drama. He plays with the association of ideas but his riddles are not meant to be solved. His purpose, if he has one—and he seriously wonders whether he does, whether there is anything more to his work than his own stubborn pleasure in covering the clean, white pages of a notebook with black letters—is to immerse the reader in a shifting sequence of states of being and mysterious mental processes, repeating, amplifying, and transforming certain elusive themes that are always accompanied by the counterpoint of memory. We inhabit his stories as if they were music. "Furthermore, I will ask you to interrupt your reading of this book as many times as possible," a character of his writes, in a story titled "Gangster Philosophy," "and perhaps—almost certainly—what you think during those intervals will be the best part of the book."

Several years after their marriage, his fourth wife fell and broke her arm and was hospitalized. He didn't visit her in the hospital, but took advantage of her absence to move all his things out of her house.

In 1939, during a tour through the Argentine province of Buenos Aires, he gave a concert in the provincial city of Chivilcoy. Thirty-eight years later, in an apartment in Paris, on the rue Saint-Honoré, Julio Cortázar read a letter Felisberto had written from Chivilcoy, dated December 26, 1939, and Cortázar remembered that he himself had lived in Chivilcoy from 1939 to 1944, teaching at the local college. Concerts were few and far between in that "run-down city on the pampas" where "almost nothing ever happened," and he certainly wouldn't have missed Felisberto's performance, but it was summer in the Southern Hemisphere and he had returned to Buenos Aires for a few weeks.

"Felisberto, do you realize," Cortázar wrote to Felisberto, years after Felisberto's death, "do you realize how close we were? Only a few days earlier and I would have been there and heard you! Or rather I would have heard you and the 'Mandolión' and the third musician, even though I didn't know anything about you as a writer then; that would happen much later, in 1947, with *No One Lit the Lamps*. And yet I believe we would have *recognized* each other in that club where everything would have projected us towards each other, and I would have invited you to my little room to offer you a *caña* and show you some books and maybe, who knows, some of the stories I was writing then and never published. Anyway, we would have talked about music and listened to the records I played on the Victrola, which scratchily emanated Mozart quartets and Bach partitas, and also, of course, Gardel and Jelly Roll Morton and Bing Crosby—all otherwise unknown in Chivilcoy. I know we would have become friends. Just imagine, Felisberto, what would have grown out of that meeting and the effect it could have had on our future, only I had to leave just then for Buenos Aires, and you had to go and choose that gap as the moment to give your concert."

The characters in one of his earliest stories, "Genealogy" (1926), are an infinite horizontal line and a circumference which rolls along the line. Approached by a vigorous triangle, the circumference gradually takes on the form of an ellipse. The triangle changes into a moderate pentagon, then a merry quadrilateral. In its passion, the quadrilateral catches up with the ellipse and a series of fleeting eclipses occur, followed by the final, eternal eclipse, when "in a vertigo of velocity" the ellipse is enclosed in the quadrilateral and they spend the rest of their young lives like that. When they die, they open out to form two horizontal lines which unite and are superimposed on the original one. The story concludes, "And thus, slowly, space was filled with many infinite horizontal lines." (Like a sheet of music.)

Luckily, his fascination with abstraction eventually took on other forms. Decades later, in a foreword to an Italian translation, Italo Calvino wrote, "What is most astonishing in [Felisberto's] writing is the rendering of the physicality of objects and people." "*Et comme il sait humaniser un domaine extrëmement imprévu et singulier!*" Jules Supervielle had already commented.

His formal education ended when he was fifteen; he had decided to dedicate himself entirely to the piano, and there were also some difficulties about passing exams. (One of his stories, describing a love affair, alludes to the twenty-two days between May 19 and June 6, and we will never know if he really thought that twenty-two was the correct number, or was purposely evincing his disdain for numbers, or was making a tacit but deliberate comment on the experience of love.) But yes, he read Proust, and Rilke, and Freud. At the age of twenty he began attending cultural soirées hosted by Carlos Vaz Ferreira, the leading Uruguayan philosopher of the day who contended that philosophy would not truly be born until philosophers began including their own psychology, their own soul, their own thought processes in their work. (Vaz Ferreira "saw writing as a productive gesture rather than a finished product," writes Roberto Echevarren in a study of Felisberto's work.)

Like his fellow *rioplatense* Jorge Luis Borges—who in 1943 became the first person to publish Felisberto's work outside of Uruguay when he selected one of his stories for inclusion in the legendary Buenos Aires journal *Sur*—Felisberto was a great reader of philosophy: Vaz Ferreira, of course, but also Bergson (*Matter and Memory*), Whitehead, many others.

Inevitably, Felisberto found his way to the secret tunnel, open only to poets, that connects Montevideo and Paris. One of the earliest to pass through it was Isidor Ducasse, the self-styled Comte de Lautréamont and quintessential 19th-century *poète maudit* who grew up in Montevideo where his father was a secretary at the French consulate. Jules Supervielle, another French poet born in Uruguay, took the same route but then returned to Montevideo in 1942, fleeing the war. He met Felisberto there and became intrigued with his work. In 1946 Supervielle pursuaded the French government to give Felisberto a grant that allowed him to spend almost two years writing in Paris, where Supervielle and the French essayist Roger Caillois took him under their wing.

In Paris, he was astonished by the sight of couples kissing openly in the streets and the Metro, and annoyed by the cold winter, the bureaucracy and the long lines. "But," he wrote to a friend, "you are assaulted from morning to night here by a madness for seeing. The narrow, silent streets make you feel that the sound of your footsteps will collapse the houses. . . ." Two of his stories were published in French, and there were plans for a French publication of his anthology of stories. Jean Paulhan, longtime editor of the *Nouvelle Revue Française,* expressed his admiration for Felisberto's work; Supervielle gave a talk about it to the Paris Pen Club; and in the Sorbonne's Amphitheatre Richelieu Felisberto read one of his stories and—at the insistance of Supervielle, who delighted in his spontaneous storytelling—extemporized an account of a trip across Uruguay. This heady interlude filled him with mad thoughts of success and popularity.

By 1948, he was back at work in Montevideo at the Uruguayan Authors Association. Roger Caillois's wife, Yvette, who was supposed to render his anthology into French, never completed the translation. "You cannot imagine," Felisberto wrote to Supervielle in 1952, "how greatly even a little of your presence is missed in Montevideo."

His pursuit of happiness was avid and skeptical. Of the grandly metaphysical hero of an early story he wrote, "He tried to anesthetize himself and let epochs go by, to see whether progress had rid men of pain or whether, when one pain diminished, another, different pain was born and raised the pressure of pain to the same level as before. It may be, as well, that if there were less pain there would be less pleasure . . . average levels of pleasure and pain wouldn't change, and it would make no difference which epoch you were born in." Nevertheless, he was drawn toward the past.

In a 1954 letter to Reina Reyes, his fourth wife, he outlined a story he had just "discovered": Someone has had the idea of changing the Nobel Prize so as to give the writer who wins it "a more authentic happiness," and prevent the fame and money currently attendant upon it from disrupting his life and work. The new idea consists of not revealing the identity of the winner even to the winner himself, but using the prize money to assemble a group of people—psychologists, for the most part—who instead would secretly study and promote the writer and his work for the duration of his life. The conferral of the prize would be publically announced only after the winner's death.

He was immune to any literary school or established definition of what literature was or should be, any received idea or prefabricated phrase. His stories, he said, were like rare and mysterious plants that grew and blossomed within him. "Most certain of all is that I don't know how I write my stories," a brief note titled "A False Explanation of My Stories" concluded, "for each one has its own strange life. But I do know that they spend their lives quarreling with my consciousness in an effort to avoid the foreigners it recommends to them."

"Felisberto Hernández is a writer like no other; like no European, nor any Latin American," wrote Italo Calvino.

Polished eloquence was not his goal, and his prose is often strangely inchoate. In 1945, in one of the earliest reviews of Felisberto's work, Emir Rodríguez Monegal pointed out its "ambiguities of logical exposition and imprecise syntax," its style "full of flaws and colloquialisms," and concluded that these arose from "the need to create mystery and attest to its importance in confrontation with the unrealizable past." Felisberto worked obsessively on everything he wrote, sometimes, for years on end, and achieved the effect he was striving for. The quality of the printed page he most cherished was its silence. He wrote towards silence, towards a world enveloped in silence, like a thick blanket of invisible snow.

His friends arranged for the publication of most of his books; his friends arranged for his concerts. In 1955, nine of his friends, including Vaz Ferreira, wrote to the Uruguayan government to request that "Felisberto Hernández be offered a modest and dignified employment so that his creative process can be uninterrupted."

Some of the things that attracted his attention:

The two halves of an open casement window, facing each other in perfect parallel.

A black cat or dog.

Hands in general; the sight of his own "knotty black" hand, and the thought of it entwined with the white hand of a certain woman.

A white dress.

Tree-lined streets, and a view through tall tree trunks into the distance.

Shifting patterns of light over the surfaces of things.

Balconies, raised platforms, upper tiers.

Blindness.

Dimly lit rooms. The moment when a light goes out.

Hats in general, and the shadows cast by hat brims. Veils.

Trains and streetcars.

A glimpse of his own face in two mirrors that met at a right angle, showing him half his head attached to the ear of the other half.

Modern architecture, which he loathed.

Certain metaphors recur. He would compare flesh to clouds. He would compare himself to an empty room.

He was fond of his private system of shorthand notation and used it for some of his own writing. Those pages, found among his papers after his death, have never been deciphered.

The movies of his youth—in which people gesticulated at each other and moved their lips, but their voices remained forever inaudible—played on inside his head. When he describes a dream as having "the jumbled quality of an old movie," he could be speaking of his own work. Jason Wilson has called the persona of some of his stories "Chaplinesque," and Felisberto can almost be said to have written in black and white, though there are vivid instants of color, especially the color green. In an early story, he remembers having taken pleasure in "a strip of green felt, visible against the piano case where the keys ended."

In 1964, just before he died, he was told he had a form of leukemia known colloquially in Spanish as *purpura*—purple. Death interested him; his only fear was that the disease would turn his body purple and render it unfit for display at his wake. When he died, his body was so large it wouldn't fit through the door but had to be taken out the window, like a piano.

Then, at the cemetery, another difficulty arose: the grave that had been prepared was too small for the enormous coffin. Angel

Rama was one of the hundred or so funeral-goers who stood around the open pit in silence, under the blazing midafternoon sun, listening to the muffled thud of spade against earth and the grave digger's labored breathing as he worked fiercely to widen the hole. Rama noticed that some of the sweat dripping off the grave digger's body splashed onto the lid of the coffin and trickled along its polished surface.

A lifetime earlier, in his first book *Fulano de tal* (Mr. So-and-So)—twenty-one paragraphs long—under the heading "Things to Read on the Streetcar," Felisberto had devised a "Simplistic Theory of Fat Souls":

"I'm thinking up a new theosophical theory of reincarnation. The disproportion between the number of inhabitants who are born and the number who die must be explained. I believe that the thin have thin souls and the fat have fat souls. When a thin man dies his soul is born again in the soul of a single child, but a fat man is reincarnated in four, five or even more little souls at once."

—Esther Allen

LANDS OF MEMORY

AROUND THE TIME OF CLEMENTE COLLING

I'M NOT SURE WHY CERTAIN memories of mine want to come into Colling's story. They don't seem to have much to do with him. Descriptions of that period in my childhood and the family who introduced me to Colling aren't important enough to the subject to justify their appearance here. The logic of the connecting thread would be very weak. Yet for some reason I don't understand those memories keep turning up in this story. And they persist, so I've chosen to grant them my attention.

I'll also have to write many things I know very little about; it even strikes me that impenetrability is intrinsic to them. Perhaps when we think we know them we stop knowing that we don't know them, because their existence is inevitably obscure, and that must be one of their qualities.

But I don't believe I must write only what I know. I must also write the other things.

The memories come, but they don't keep still. And some very foolish memories clamor for attention, too. I don't yet know whether, despite their childishness, these have some important connection to the other memories, or what meanings and reflections memories exchange among themselves. Some seem to protest the selection the intellect claims to make among them. And they reappear unexpectedly, as if to ask for new meanings, or to make new and fleeting jokes, or to inflect everything with a different purpose.

The streetcars that run along Calle Suárez—which I can see from the inside, on one of their wicker seats, just as readily as from the sidewalk, watching them—are red and white, a yellowish white. Not long ago I walked through that area again. Just before the curve the Number 42 makes when it goes down Asencio and turns onto Suárez I saw the sun flashing on the tracks, as it used to. The streetcar's wheels emit a deafening screech when it runs along those tracks. (But in memory the noise is muted and pleasant, calling up other memories in turn.) A fence also runs along the curve, and that same fence surrounds a traffic circle overgrown with wisteria.

There are many estates in that area. Along Calle Suárez there wasn't much else. A lot of them are subdivided now. Modern times— the same times when I was journeying through other places and in some way coming to be another person—broke up those estates, killed trees and built many small houses, new but already dingy and wretched, and shops that huddle together with little heaps of merchandise at their doors. An auction has taken a capricious nibble out of one grand, baronial estate—a little square bite in one side that has left it dolefully incomprehensible. The new owner has made it his business to give that little square the look of a garish patch sewn onto the landscape: a small, modern house, clumsy and pretentious, heaves its unpleasant disproportions at the eye there, ridiculing the beautiful majesty, now offended and humiliated, that the mansion in the background retains. That mansion is much like the ones I would see on Sundays when I went to the Biógrafo Olivos—the closest movie house—in my early adolescence, when that style of house was young and from its front door a grand stairway would flow, spreading out like the train of a bridal gown, its edges unfurling, but with a lot of rolled-up edge still left at the base, on top of which a large planter would sit, with or without plants—preferably plants with big leaves that would hang down all around. At the foot of that stairway, just starting to make her long, languid way up, was La Borelli or La Bertini. And the things those women would do as they walked up a flight of stairs! Today we would think they'd been filmed with a *ralentisseur*, but in those days I thought that that particular number of movements scattered across that particular quantity of time, with so much meaning that was so enigmatic to my almost childish mind, must pertain to the secrets of very intelligent adults. And I wanted to be older in order to understand those secrets; I aspired to understand what I was already beginning to feel with an obscure and indolent anguish. It was something that those movements covered over with an all too serious dignity, something which, perhaps, could only be profaned by the same vastly superior art the woman was putting to use. (And I thought about profaning it.) Perhaps she could be reached by a mental effort as great and a flight as high as that of bees in pursuit of their queen.

In the meantime, a long gown covered the woman, stairway and all.

But let's go back to the route of the Number 42.

After the streetcar passed in front of the little lot—that patch on the baronial mansion—the two tall, swaying palm trees that rose behind that modern, claptrap house stayed in my eyes for a moment, in precise detail. Thinking over the fleeting vision of those palm trees, I recognized them and remembered how they had once looked when I was a child and there was no patch on the estate. A literary man of that time would have something to write about if he could see them now behind that ugly little house! The pair of elderly palms nodded their great shaggy, drooping heads meaningfully, like two faithful old servants discussing the misfortune of their masters who've come down in the world. And when that reflection came to me, I remembered how the people of that time expressed life, and how they reflected it in their art, and what their artistic predilections were. (But I don't want these reflections to engulf me right now: I want to stay with the Number 42.)

Then an immense, horrible billboard caught my eye. (I won't say which billboard so as not to give its owner any further publicity. And if he paid me would I? And thoughts like that kept emerging: wasn't it a son of the baronial mansion who sold off that piece of the estate to settle a shameful debt?)

I was feeling sad and pessimistic. I thought about the many new things there are, and how insolently some of them burst upon us. Someone was delivering a sales pitch to me on the feeling for whatever is new—and for all that is new—as a marvelous human necessity. He spoke impetuously, though he conceded a moment's mocking irony to my old attachments.

He was in a rush and soon turned his unpleasant head away and took his whole person off somewhere else. But he left something grayish in my sadness; he discredited it for me, made me doubt even the dignity of my own sadness, and soiled it with a new, unknown substance that was unexpectedly disagreeable, like a strange taste suddenly noticed in tainted food.

Nevertheless, there are some places among the estates that have few "modifications," where you can feel as sad as you like for a little while. Then memories begin climbing slowly down from the cobwebs they've made for themselves in the favorite corners of childhood.

Once, a long time ago, I recalled those memories arm in arm with a woman. This last time, a grubby, weeping child came out of one of the houses. Now I begin to think of the right that certain new things have to live, and I begin to feel a new bias. (Perhaps I'm going too far; perhaps the bias in favor of anything new is expanding to overtake everything, as it overtook the deliverer of the sales pitch. After all, it takes only a slight bias and immediately we find a thousand theories served up to justify anything at all. Moreover, we can very easily switch among causes to be justified, however contradictory they may be, for there are theories with a touch of exoticism, theories of suggestive mystery, theories of a naturalist origin, theories with philosophical depth, etcetera.)

Now I remember a place where the Number 42 goes at top speed, when it crosses Calle Gil. One of that street's broad sidewalks crashes against my eyes with a spinning jolt. On that sidewalk, when I was about eight, I dropped a bottle of wine. Then I gathered up the shards and took them home, a block away. At home they laughed a great deal and asked why I'd brought the shards back: what was I going to do with them? That logic was very difficult for me—it still is—because I hadn't brought home the shattered pieces to prove I had broken the bottle; they would have believed me anyway. I don't know whether I brought them so they could see them, or why.

If we walk toward Suárez on our way back from where my house used to be on Calle Gil, before we get to the corner we'll pass a very old brick wall, blackened and blanketed with many different shades of green moss. Behind the wall, a grown-up will see—while I hop up and down, trying to see—turkeys among some trees and a henhouse made of whitewashed chicken wire. Once a very deep pit was dug there, and a madman would go down into it because he didn't want to hear any noise while he was reading. Continuing along the sidewalk we reach the house at the corner, which has many windows facing Calle Gil. But the last window before Suárez is painted on the wall. And behind the painted window is the room where the madman lived. Only with an effort did it suggest terrifying things to me; between its painted bars a sky blue color was painted, and the fake window didn't inspire any dark thoughts. Nevertheless, the madman was once on the point of killing his mother—who was paralyzed and always sat in a chair—with an ax. Fortunately the three daughters arrived just in time. After that the madman spent a while in confinement and then another while with the three of them. He was a very gentle, cultured, and affable person. Once he gave me a chocolate mouse, and I stared gratefully up at his goatee, which was short and combed into two points. But the women! How nobly ideal they were! Through those three long-lived women I was able to reach out my hand to a large portion of the past century. Leafing through magazines of that period, it wouldn't be at all hard to find an "original" illustrator who had drawn a cigarette letting out a cloud of smoke with a silhouette like theirs emerging from it: the narrowest possible waist, the ample bosom, the throat enclosed by little stays that held the white fabric in place. (At that time my attention was caught by things that lay on a slant, and in that house there were many: the whitewashed squares of the henhouse's chicken wire, the white checks of fabric at the neckline, held in place by stays, the courtyard with its great black-and-white flagstones, the cushions on the beds.) And another sizable mass was perched on the head, like a large hat, but it was made up of the hair that grew from the head—or else it   was   half-personal hair and half-purchased hair (the bosom was also generally half and half). On top of the hair sat the actual hat, usually immense, and on top of the hat, feathers—from the turkeys in the back, or from other birds, though I don't think from hens ever, unless they were dyed. The hats were usually weighed down with fruit—grapes, I think—and were held in place by extremely long pins with large heads made of metal or colored stones or tortoiseshell. The pins pierced through the entirety of the coiffure and the hat—with its flowers, fruit or whatever else—and reappeared on the other side, sticking out a long way still, and ending in an aggressive point. From the brim of the hat to the neckline, a piece of tulle, like a mosquito net, was tightly stretched, leaving the face behind it in provocative and appealing penumbra; the face, in turn, was covered with powder. The spectator's contemplation could tarry a good while over this fantastical apparition. As a boy I once put one of those display cases—mosquito net and all—on my head, and as I walked around I remembered a ride I once took in a closed carriage from which I could see out through little curtains without being seen.

One night we went with my mother to the home of the three long-lived ladies. In the half-light of the entryway we walked across the great square black-and-white flagstones. There was no inner door and we could see the big plants in the middle of the courtyard. We were shown into a small parlor that took its light from what little there was in the street and occasionally from the illuminated squares of the Number 42's windows passing through the dimness at top speed. The reflected windows, too, lay at a slant as they moved across the floor, and were even more slanted when they crawled up the wall. The three women's camaraderie as they conversed was so frank and sincere, they took such joy in their courtesies, the voices of all three joined together and rose so high that it put the general shadowiness out of mind; there didn't seem to be any such thing. In addition to living in darkness, they were all nearsighted. One of them, the one who was said to do the cooking, sat in the darkest corner; her pale, oval face dotted with moles—like a badly peeled potato with the black eyes showing—could hardly be seen. Another was in the habit of rubbing her fists hard against her cheeks to bring out their color—she was the one who went out to pay calls. All three were very thin. And I realized that at my house they were right when they said that the three ladies—during intervals of animated conversation and especially when laughing—made a very loud noise by taking in air between their teeth. Then I noticed that the sound was so loud even the Number 42 going by at top speed didn't drown it out. But I wished I hadn't been made aware of it because then I had to pay too much attention to that and couldn't go on feeling other things. And I liked to go and be in that house.

In my family there was a distant aunt, as old as the long-lived ladies and also a spinster. And that aunt called them "the hissers." This irritated me a great deal. And not because I was in love with any of them. (Though I always found myself strongly predisposed to fall in love with any teacher I had, or any friend of my mother's who came to the house. But not the long-lived ladies.) Like my mother, those women inspired my affection by the nobility of their feelings and the pleasure they took in the time they spent with us. Perhaps they were so happy at those moments because the other hours of their lives were occupied with many things, those strange, infinite tasks that responsible people generally have, and many moral qualms and many sorrows. The hissing was the most striking thing, but that doesn't mean it should be dwelt upon more than all the rest. Not to mention the fact that calling them by that name created a false synthesis of them, a synthesis that didn't include all the rest but concealed it to some degree, and when you thought of them the first thing to appear in memory was the hissing, which was discussed far too much. I laughed without wanting to, then silently raged.

Many years later I realized that I wanted to rebel against the injustice of insisting too much on the things that are the most striking without being the most important. If I could get past the clamor that a certain critique makes in some part of our thinking, keeping us from feeling or forming less easily solidified ideas, if I could manage not to yield without a struggle to the convenience of certain syntheses—those formed without much in the way of prior content—then I arrived at a mystery that awoke in me another quality of interest in the things that happened. But at that time I was entering into the mystery of those women, astonished that although, in the things they spoke of with my mother, they displayed liveliness and discernment, as well as a breadth of knowledge and common sense that enabled them to observe a great deal about other people, they, the three of them, did not perceive other things that for us seemed very easy to see. And it wasn't just the hissing or the habit of rubbing clenched fists over cheekbones. The mystery began with the observation that, mixed in with the things they understood, were other things that didn't correspond to what we're used to encountering in reality. And that gave rise to an attitude of expectation: there was always the hope that from one moment to the next something strange would happen, one of those things that they didn't know was out of the ordinary.

When we became good friends, they showed us into the other rooms. The place no one could ever go was out back where the turkeys were; that place was defended by some extremely fierce geese who instantly went after any intruder, making an incredible racket and pecking him if he didn't get out of there quickly; they even used to run after the three women and tear their dresses. After crossing the courtyard, you entered a room that had a floor made of wide planks. When you stepped on them, the planks would give a little, and your footsteps were automatically answered by the knickknacks, still invisible in the gloom. The ancient, paralyzed mother was sitting in another room, though she was in full view because the large doors connecting the two rooms were wide open and her white head and white shawl were easy to make out in the darkness. What caught the eye even more was the constant, regular movement of her head, which reminded you, irreverently, of a wind-up toy. All the women were talking loudly and I began to recognize the objects in the room; they seemed as cordial and kindly as the ladies. The mystery of that place wasn't crouched in shadows or in silence. It lay, rather, in certain turns, rhythms or bends that suddenly took the conversation to places that didn't seem to be part of reality. And that also happened with certain incidents.

The elderly lady was more than seventy years old and had been paralyzed for many of those years. One of her sons, who killed himself—not the madman—had played an important role at the side of a politician they all admired with patriotic fervor. After the son's death, the politician came to visit them, and she, the elderly lady, almost eighty years old, composed some lines of poetry to welcome him. Poems and even common prose were generally difficult for me, but those lines were far more so; they ascended to regions I had no notion of whatsoever. Nor did they refer to the kind of patriotic themes I heard about in school, which I was used to not understanding. Near the end, the words seemed to come down to earth, to a terrain where something could be grasped; the old lady spoke very vaguely of the bliss she felt at the existence in the world of this being: the politician.

In a closet, the long-lived ladies had a doll, as long and thin as they were, but black, with kinky locks made of astrakhan. They would display the doll but didn't let anyone touch it because it had belonged to a niece of theirs who had died. The first time we were in their inner rooms they suddenly fell silent in great tension because my younger sister had touched the tail of a large parrot sitting very still on a pedestal. We thought there was some danger. But it turned out that they had loved the parrot very much, and now they were keeping it, stuffed and mounted. After that we got used to this family "totem" which they spoke to as if it were alive. The one who did the cooking answered questions for it, imitating its voice like a ventriloquist.

It was there that I met a musician, the women's nephew, whom they called "El nene"—"the youngster." He was blind and must have been about eighteen years old. And very tall. Behind a pair of dark glasses, his eyes moved in the most impressive way; they stuck out so far and were so startlingly large that they looked as if they were about to jump out of his head. His eyelids had grown and stretched, but still couldn't pocket the entirety of those eyeballs away. Seeing them continually moving outside their sockets was disturbing, and brought to mind the movement of a cow's eyes seen in profile. To say that his eyes were the size of eggs would be no exaggeration at all; this was suggested not only by their dimension but also by their oval shape. I was once told the name of that disease and then forgot it. But what bothered me most was that the doctor had predicted he would die at the age of twenty-two; those eyes would pop out of their sockets. Once, a doctor even told me—perhaps driven to it by my persistence in asking what time of year it would happen—that the event would occur in March, more or less. Fortunately I know that he lived past his fortieth birthday.

One night, invited by his aunts—the long-lived ladies—we went to Elnene's house and heard him play the piano. It made an extraordinary impression on me. Through him, I had my initiation into classical music. He played a Mozart sonata and for the first time I experienced the seriousness of music. And the pleasure—perhaps mingled with considerable vanity—of thinking that I was connecting myself to something of legitimate value. I also felt the pride of being included in an aesthetically superior aspect of life: it was a luxury for me to understand and be within this thing, which belonged only to intelligent people. But then, when he played one of his own compositions, a nocturne, I experienced a pleasure that was truly mine: it filled me up with pleasure. For the first time I experienced the coincidence of someone else having created something with an oddness and wit to it that I felt to be my own, or that I would have wanted as my own. The melody suddenly descended to a strange note that suggested a passion and at the same time a rightness, and it was as if I'd seen a companion doing something very close to my way of thinking and my life, as if the two of us found ourselves in agreement on a predilection; it was like the complicity of two classmates telling each other about similar amorous escapades. I had found classmates for other things, but a friend with whom I could share an image of love was a secret of life we could forever be reaching toward with hidden delight in further surprises—the kind of surprises that depend largely on our own hands.

This was much lovelier than my way of playing. And I thought

I was so original when I played to please myself, compressing or
stretching out a melody as much as I liked! And nothing less than
the *Song of Margarita*! Which was precisely what I played one
night when the long-lived ladies were visiting my house, and they
said, "But how he enjoys playing!" and "Look how lovely the
music is!" And then there was the night, so immensely distant—
yet so near in the sense of things and of life that I couldn't say
what this strange recognition of myself is or where it resides—
when I played a mazurka called—mortification!—"Gorjeo de
Pájaros" or "Warbling Birds." And how we laughed because my
little sister—four years old, the one who touched the parrot's tail—
said very distinctly, "*Mamá, decile que toque gorjeo de lechones*"—
"Mama, tell him to play warbling pigs." And then my other sister,
the older one, recited "Pobre María": a poor unfortunate girl,
thrashed by her stepmother, has run away from home and spent
the night outdoors in winter, without warm clothes; finding herself
in front of a door with a sign on it, she's afraid it might be the
"penitentiary." But at last she discovers that it is an orphanage.
Then she knocks, the door opens, and she gives thanks to the Vir-
gin. My sister was standing in front of the dining room door as she
recited, and just when she said, "footsteps, they open, and come
out"—without anyone suspecting anything, not even my sister
herself—the dining room door opened and I appeared, to give
more reality to the scene. The idea had come to me while she was
reciting; I'd left the parlor on tiptoe and gone around another way.
The consequences were disastrous; all of them, who had been very
moved until then, were now laughing as well, at the same time as
they almost wept, and they were furious, too: the joke had robbed
"the work" of all its effect.

I was twelve or thirteen years old then. A cousin of mine, also
distant, played the piano (*The Prayer of Moses, Argentina Weeps for
Thee*—a nocturne dedicated to a fallen aviator—etc.). She was very
pretty and at least twice my age. (Another secret love, but with the

aggravating factor that we were far too close, not to mention my shyness and my fear that she would think I had misinterpreted our closeness. And she was full of mockery, too.)

One hot, sunlit afternoon during Carnival, four tall women in costume appeared at our house and we soon detected the long-lived ladies. But since there were only three of them, we had to guess the fourth, who didn't speak a word. Well, it turned out to be the little blind boy, Elnene. He often visited our house after that, and met my cousin there. (Fatal coincidence: he, too, fell in love with her.) Once when he danced with her he left a piece of paper in her hand. It was the lyrics to an *estilo* he had composed for her. How I envied him! He had played the *estilo* before, but of course without saying who he was dedicating it to. This was the tenor of the lyrics (he had sung them, as well):

One night I dreamed you told me
Your voice choked with feeling
Yours is my soul, yours is my life,
Yours is all my heart.

The distant aunt was named Petrona. She would always laugh at the long-lived ladies, imitating one of them by making herself "hard and frowning," and constantly reminding us of the words that same one would say to her nephew: "Nene, play your nocturne." As usual, I raged inwardly. But one day I began to think that Petrona, despite not feeling the nocturne, not understanding or being included in it, or even aspiring to any situation or aesthetic state such as the one we were enjoying, did in her own way feel something of what was happening in those who were hearing and enjoying the moment of art. Like many people without intellectual cultivation—she barely read the newspaper—she felt a tension in her spirit when she was among "educated" people; you could sense her batteries becoming overcharged at those moments, and whenever there was a chance to laugh she would let out a peal of violent laughter, more convulsive and lasting than anyone else's. This also happened whenever the conversation touched on a person who happened to be in a somewhat difficult situation or one that tended toward the absurd. The affinity between Petrona's state and that of the person in question had a direct influence on her storage batteries and she waited with repressed impatience—even if she herself didn't know it—for the chance to let out intermittent explosions of laughter. In fact, her convulsions of laughter were cause for much concern because her efforts to contain them were so evident. She sucked in her laughter, and only half choked back her convulsions—someone used to say she "decapitated" them. Perhaps her anxious efforts to hold in her laughter by pressing desperately on all her muscular brakes sprang from a desire not to "make a fool of herself," not to make a display of coarse laughter. In this struggle with her laughter she presented a strange and impressive spectacle. There was more to this spectacle, however, than simply the reaction of a person we call sane and healthy, who offers us a great wealth of energy, but whose energies, on coming into contact with a higher sphere than the one she's used to, turn in on themselves, checked by modesty, because she perceives the difference in milieu and wants to hide her background (or because, knowing her background is being detected and that she is making a spectacle of herself, she finds it mortifying to enter this different sphere). For Petrona's mystery also concealed a certain persistent tendency to brutal mockery. While on the one hand she was generous, self-sacrificing, and constant in her care and efforts on our behalf—she was already living in the house before we were born—on the other, she was constantly playing jokes on us and some of the jokes she came up with were cruel. One night when I was three and had been left alone with the light on, I saw something appear through the gray bedroom door that stood ajar, something like the long black leg of a spider, moving forward, and it was her; she had put a black stocking over her hand and arm and poked it through, wriggling. I remember very well how I felt.

At home they used to say they thought I would go mad that night.

Picking up a toad between two fingers she would show me its white underbelly. I was afraid; she herself had told me that toads will shoot out a powerful spurt of urine that hits your eyes and blinds you. One rainy night after I was in bed she came in and I saw her jerk back the blankets. Then I felt the toad's cold, viscous belly on my feet. A few nights later, my mother noticed a strange noise after the light was out; she quickly lit a match and discovered that I was sleeping with my feet and legs up, pressed tight against the wall. Now I feel again a little of my anguish at the moment the light was turned off and the lamp's wick let out its final hiccups, and in the end, when the light was almost entirely out, the last hiccup took longer to arrive but was bigger, and then everything was completely dark. Then I started seeing toads in my bed and put my legs on the wall. My mother took me to her bed and my father went to mine. When my mother was about to fall asleep I poked her with my elbow to keep her awake because I was still afraid of the toads.

Yet Petrona was very good-natured and did all she could to spoil us, indulging us in every way, from morning to night. Even during the night she would bring all of us a hot water bottle. One night, when we all came back from the theater—my little sister, the one with the parrot, must have been about four—we found our beds warm, as usual. And in my little sister's bed Petrona had also put her doll, with a little ink jar full of hot water at the doll's feet. When my older sister—the one who recited "Pobre María"—was about nine, she was scolded for always going everywhere at a run, "like a goat." Petrona told her that if she went on running like that she'd grow horns like a goat. That afternoon it was raining and they made fried cakes, and Petrona shaped the dough into a large fried horn and took it to her. After that my sister walked slowly, on tiptoe, touching her forehead.

Though Petrona hadn't cultivated an aesthetic feeling for art, she had developed an aesthetic sense of life, where certain aspects of human behavior were concerned. (Of course she wouldn't have called it an aesthetic sense. She may never have uttered the word "aesthetic.") She had some concept of what was beautiful and what was ugly, what was good and what was bad. She synthesized that concept in the expression "to make a fool of," which was what she tried to do or not to do. She had her own distinctive sensibility and certain things tickled her: hence her constant stifled laughter. And we wouldn't have been satisfied with the idea that this mockery was a secret vengeful reaction against more cultivated people. That seemed to leave something out; it fell short and couldn't give us access to the full reality of her person. There was also the idea that this mockery or delighted reaction concealed a strange temperament, and so she could not do otherwise than abandon herself continually to this tendency which she was at the same time condemned to be forever holding in check. You might say that it would be difficult to find her—in the sense of understanding her—if we used ordinary criteria or sentiments to look for her, and so we were always tempted to postpone the estimation of her we were seeking to form. She, however, quickly—immediately— formed her own estimation of everyone else. She was actually a very balanced person. (Though sometimes, the greater the appearance of equilibrium, the more surprising the madnesses and the more inscrutable the mysteries we find.) In her equilibrium, in a certain freshness she retained—never having been interfered with by any theory, aesthetic or otherwise, which might have tempted her spirit to seize onto something that might have become a small extravagance or an odd predilection—and above all in her mystery, she observed other people and detected with great ease and precision the least extravagance to which anyone abandoned himself. At a gathering devoted to art, therefore, she understood the stances that other people adopted. And therein lay her great opportunity for mockery.

It may sometimes happen that people whose feelings, memories, and predispositions lead them to bring a more or less profound, spontaneous, and sincere attitude to the moment of art fail, even so, to adopt interesting expressions or poses. Among other people—those spirits disinclined to take part in such moments in an uninterrupted and more or less profound way, either because they are preoccupied with things foreign to art, because they feel beneath or above it just then, or because their temperaments or circumstances don't allow them to spend any time on art, ever— among these people, there are always a few who will take advantage of the opportunity to adopt seductive, suggestive, appealing poses. They may even strike these poses while taking some note of their circumstances, and in the capricious shifts of their attention they may acquire a pose that is related to the emotions art is giving rise to, or they may even allow art to possess them at scattered intervals that do not disrupt the composition of their poses. But other very strange things may happen, as well. There may be people who experience the moment of art with dignity and give themselves over to it with all the profundity of their souls, but who are prone nevertheless to extravagant poses. They can't possibly be accused of trying to profit from their poses, or of deliberately attempting to attract attention. But it is possible that in their adolescence, when they felt for the first time that art was sublime and the moment of experiencing it solemn, they dreamed of themselves in a stance that was adolescent, and that stance remained with them, as if asleep or forgotten. And later, whenever that sublime moment and solemn state reappeared, it would bring, together with that first emotion, the movements and poses art had suggested to them when they dreamed that initial dream of themselves, out of which, innocently, artlessly, they created the rites and spiritual garments for the ceremony of art. Though their aesthetic sensibility may have enlarged and they may have become aware that their pose was extravagant, perhaps they couldn't think much about themselves any longer, for at the moment of experiencing art they needed a more profound dream. And so the pose would remain on their surface—and they would have no mirror or consciousness to see it in. If that were the case, these gestures and postures were born and lived in these souls as other gestures were born and lived among tribes of primitive men, threading through their whole lives like a retinue of traditions maintained with ecstatic fidelity.

It would be almost pointless to take one of these people aside—however close a friend he was—and tell him his pose was extravagant, for we would be profaning rituals that have strange and particular meanings. And the moment we began to hear music, art would invite us to ease up on the brakes of self-criticism, however forewarned we might be; a kind of conventional freedom to relate the feeling of art to our own sentimental history would set in, and we would freely and justifiably relax our muscles and abandon our consciousness—as long as the abandon wasn't exaggerated, and there was no evidence of a covert attempt to achieve an original abandon. Anyone who observes the moment when he passes into the state brought about by art will see how naturally the boundaries he was living within a moment before dissolve bit by bit.

Some people must have known their poses were observed; distancing themselves from their present company, they would settle into a neutral but comfortable posture and calmly abandon themselves to listening. (Others, in imitation of them, would act as if they were getting ready to go to sleep.)

All of this tickled Petrona's sensibilities. And while some people who understood very little about art concealed their incompre-

hension—or tried to understand—by referring far too often to an-
ecdotes or to the attitudes of artists, in an attempt to *deduce* art,
Petrona dedicated herself exclusively and frankly to the observation of postures. And the bubbling, half-restrained laughter welled
up again.

I had gone to Las Piedras, the little blind boy's house, with my
mother, and at dinner I said something that embarrassed and confused everyone. People were saying that my mother had taught me
very good manners. At that time I was often full of nervous agitation and just as often overwhelmed by fatigue, often tremendously
excited and just as often inert and half-asleep. I, too, charged up my
batteries and then discharged them all at once, but usually on some
insignificant thing and to everyone's great bewilderment. And
when the subject was of real interest, I would suddenly seem slack,
distracted, lost on the moon. I was as likely to be shy to the point of
anguish as surprisingly violent and audacious. But consistently
awkward. When dinner was over—those people were as good, kind
and profoundly noble as the long-lived ladies—and we all stood up,
I prepared to give voice to our gratitude in some brilliant way. And I
said: "Thanks very much, though it isn't much . . ." And thus
trailed off, without ending, the phrase by which I had wanted to explain that simply thanking them was little or nothing compared to
so much kind attention. Through the general disconcertion that en-
sued came some incoherent stammering—offers of more food, perhaps. My mother was dismayed and I was surrounded by a luminous redness that came from a large, fringed scarlet lampshade with
a very bright light inside.

We didn't leave that friendly house until the next afternoon,
after the purpose of our stay there had been fulfilled: I was introduced to Clemente Colling. He was the blind boy's professor of
piano and harmony. Between themselves, the long-lived ladies and
Elnene had arranged this meeting.

Clemente Colling was known as "The organist at the church of

Los Vascos" or "The blind man who plays for the Basques," etc.
His reputation was based on that. Some time before our meeting
I'd been taken to a piano concert he gave at the Verdi Institute. It
was one of the first concerts I ever attended. My enthusiasm and
my mania for arriving at performances far too early put us at the
door of the concert hall long before it opened. Later, leaning on
the balustrade of the upper tier, I began to feel the dreaming silence that sets in before a concert, when there is still a long time to
go before the start and the first whisperings and dry scrapings of
chairs deepen the silence; when you are waiting to listen, but there
is more to see than to hear, and the spirit, without knowing it,
works as it waits, works almost as if in a dream, letting things
come, waiting for them and watching them with profound, childlike distraction; when you make a sudden effort to imagine what is
to come and scrutinize the program for the hundredth time; when
you review your life and your illusions venture forth, and you feel
the anguish of having no place anywhere in the world and vow to
achieve a place for yourself; when you dream of someday attracting
the attention of others and feel a certain sad resentment because
you haven't yet done so; when you lose all common sense and
dream a future that makes your scalp tingle and numbs your hair, a
future you would never confess to anyone because you see yourself
all too clearly: and this is the innermost secret of anyone who has
any modesty—and it may be the deepest part of the aesthetic sense
of life—for when you don't know what you are capable of, then
you don't know, either, if your dream is mere vanity or if it is
pride.

Looking at the stage, I suddenly felt the silence to be like the silence of a wake. The large piano was entirely white. Black pianos
have never suggested anything funereal to me, but that white piano
had something about it of a child's wake.

A lot of people had come in and the murmuring grew much

louder. Then my heart rose as well, but all at once: the lights of the concert hall went off. Still more time passed. Then, instead of a single man appearing on the stage, there were two; I hadn't thought that, Colling being blind, it was natural for someone to lead him to the piano. But they stopped before reaching the piano and Colling performed a strange bow; at first he seemed to face forward and then he turned to one side. Years later he told me this was a very elegant way of bowing that he learned in Paris. Once he was seated at the piano he spoke with a smile to the man who'd walked onstage with him. The man left, and Colling coughed and raised his hand to his mouth; he had a peculiar way of bringing his fingers together. His gray head, hair slicked down and parted on one side, was shiny on top and shadowy below. All I can remember is the way he played a Chopin ballade—one I swore to learn—and the final number when, as promised in the program, he asked the audience for four notes, as a theme upon which to improvise.

On stage he had looked completely different from the way I'd imagined him. And at our meeting in Las Piedras, quite different from the way I'd seen him on stage.

Yet my memory of that first meeting is very vague. Many years later I decided on a whim that I wanted to remember exactly where and how he was situated, how I saw him for the first time and what he said to me in those initial moments, and I spent a few nights doing that. I tried imagining him at a certain spot in that parlor, to see if my imagination could coincide with the real place he had occupied that first time and thus make my memory clearer. I tried to invent a place for myself in that parlor, a place I might possibly have been sitting, to see if some sympathy arose between what I was imagining now and what was really there back then, for I hoped my memory would become more precise if the two things coincided. But it was useless; not only did I fail to find what I was looking for, but the parlor began to grow muddled. Then I reached the point where later impressions were getting mixed in. I deduce that he must have been sitting near the piano, and I believe I had to wait for him to give the blind boy his lesson first, and only then did we come in. I don't even remember whether I noticed, during that first meeting, that he was greatly begrimed. In all likelihood he was near the piano because I passed very close to him before sitting down to play.

I must now face the embarrassment of confessing that in those days I, too, had my nocturne. "The seed is there, but it must be tended," he told me. I recall the phrase not only for its bearing on my vanity but also because it struck me as vulgar—and because of the things I couldn't keep from thinking when I saw his head slightly tilted to one side, though he was not facing me but beside me. On the other side he was resting an elbow against his body, with his arm bent upwards, and he held his cigarette between his thumb and two fingers—raising the other fingers of that hand as if he were eating a petit four. When he spoke, he stretched or puckered the part of his face that lay between the delicate edge of his upper lip and the two pigeonholes of his nostrils, which flared out at the bottom. In the very large and mobile region beneath his nose he had two dark brown marks; only a long time later did I realize that those were stains left by the cigarette smoke that emerged from his nostrils.

Colling's phrase, which had struck me as so vulgar, made me think for a moment in a way typical of young men of that period. This way of thinking was a kind of fashion: "What do you expect of such-and-such a person if he does such-and-such a thing?" That momentous instant of disillusionment with Colling was almost the equivalent of saying, "The man who utters such a vulgarity cannot be a critic of art." "If his phrase is so vulgar, his art must be, too." It's possible that such an estimation may be correct in many cases—and that this was one of those cases—but it was undoubtedly a prefabricated way of thinking that could give rise to cruel errors and prevent you from continuing to observe or think of a person with respect. Then, too, it is a truth most obvious that in a single individual extremely contradictory things can be found. I had discovered and reflected upon this mistake that other people made not through any subtlety of observation on my part, but simply because it didn't suit me—for if all my life and my being were judged by a few incidents, it would rightly be determined that I was a complete imbecile. Also, this mistake didn't fit in with my style; I had other mistakes of my own; this was not my general way of inciting an opinion within myself, and a posture of thought that didn't coincide with my own style in mistakes made me listless and cost me a great deal of effort. Moreover, it strikes me now that if I thought Colling's phrase was vulgar—well, you should have heard my nocturne! And now I can better imagine Colling's position, having myself later heard and judged the nocturnes of others. While I may have had some vague experience at that point in my life with certain kinds of mistakes, I had no experience with music. And there I was with all my soul turned toward Colling, seduced by all that was naive and picturesque about him and by his genuinely benevolent cordiality; his heart seemed to shape itself easily and with frank spontaneity to each new turn his life took. Like everyone, he had contrived an artificial smile for the sake of courtesy; but he seemed to employ this artifice with pleasure, wanting it to be wholly natural and hoping for reasons to be sincere. I was also seduced by his erudition, his immense knowledge of music. At least to me he appeared very knowledgeable. And even though some of his feelings were all too easy to discern and some of the things that struck him as funny were inexplicable, and in spite of his artless fits of pride and the seriousness of his breathtaking lies, I started to delve into the many mysteries that began when I met him in person. I felt we were going to become closely acquainted and a friendship was going to spring up for me, a strange interchange with an exceptional figure—who was blind in the bargain. I know that even during those first moments certain insignificant

details, which may have been overly physical and objective, started
to become a mystery—but they were so strange, and their history
was so unknown! Yet later I would fit them neatly into my way
of thinking about another mystery, that of his erudition. But I
never took my ignorant audacity to the extreme of neatly fitting in
other mysteries, such as the mystery of the emotions that lay behind that erudition. Nor did I know—and I found pleasure in not
knowing—what mystery might dwell in every human being set
down here on earth, a human being like Colling, for example. I
didn't know what mystery would first surprise me, what I would
be like after having experienced it, and what it would do to my own
mystery.

On that first afternoon and many others, I kept still, watching
him. Maybe I was thrown off by the fact that he was blind, so I be-
haved as if he were deaf, as well. Maybe it disconcerted me to see
myself hidden in broad daylight before his very eyes, or perhaps he
was the one who was hiding from me behind his eyelids. Maybe he
was simply proceeding in a natural fashion that was unfamiliar to
me because I didn't know what life was like without eyesight;
maybe this was the normal reaction that people with eyesight
elicited from him. He acted like a man accustomed to the curiosity
of others, and in a strange way he and the world around him were
muddled together, for the rest of us would never be able to know
what the experience and sensation of things was like for the kind of
mind in which sight had no place.

Suddenly he started laughing, as if he'd been looking at me.
Then he told a story. Recently, at the barbershop, someone was
reading an advertisement—the next Sunday Colling was going to
play the organ at the church in Las Piedras—and the man who was
reading said to the rest, "This man Colling is going to play, they
say he's a tiger." And Colling laughed in great delight because the
man had pronounced his name so badly. Colling claimed his name
was English and was correctly pronounced by stressing the first

syllable and barely making the sound of the "g." Many people, knowing he was French, called him "Mesiu Colén." He accepted that pronunciation; it was the one used by all the French. But the man in the barbershop had pronounced the "ll" as a "y," in true Rio de la Plata fashion, as if he were saying "*pollo*"; and further-more he had put the accent on the "i" and had pronounced the "g" with the full, drawn-out, aspirated ferocity of an "h," his mouth like a wild beast baring its teeth. While this was funny, the way Colling accented his words was much stranger. Telling us about a sighted girl who had visited the Institute for the Blind and wanted to be sightless herself when she saw the little blind girls, he would say, "*y entonces la muchachita se echaba jábon en los ojos*"—"zhen ze leetle girl rubbed *so*-ap in her eyes"—dividing the word into two syllables and accenting the first, and as we laughed at the proce-dure with the soap, we were also laughing at how strange "soap" sounded when it was pronounced that way, and at the childlike oblivion in which he laughed, unaware of his mistake.

When I was first left alone with the two blind men who were con-versing, I didn't keep in mind that they were blind, and when the conversation took an unexpected turn or moved onto a more inti-mate footing it startled me that they didn't look at each other or make the movements we're used to seeing sighted people make; they were creating, before my eyes, a new set of conversational ges-tures. Their restless heads, almost continually in motion, would turn to the side, as if they were looking with their ears; but the one who was uttering words kept his face forward, toward the other's ear, and when the dialogue grew heated there was great confusion and a worrisome twitching of heads. Then they went over to the piano. But while they were discussing composition—and, in the same vein, sonorous sensations, feelings, art, and science—their conversation seemed more secret; they went to places where I had few thoughts, few experiences. Nevertheless, my expectant curi-

osity, stimulated by vague suggestions, was continually alert to the
fact that while some of my experiences managed to accompany
them down their pathways, others led me astray and left me lost
and anxious to find the two blind men once more. As night came
on—they needed no light—I followed their movements as they
dissolved into two gesturing silhouettes next to the larger silhouette of the piano. From out of a huge, abstract crate they were taking abstract toys that, for me, had color as well as sonority. But I
didn't realize that the chords I heard differed from the ones they
were hearing because mine had color; like the young girl who
rubbed soap in her eyes so she could be blind, I shifted a little for a
moment towards their religion as I listened to them—their lack of
eyesight and mutual understanding suggested something religious
to me—and thought that perhaps, in the deepest depths of what
makes us human, eyesight is superfluous. But this thought immediately struck me as horrible, and I remembered what delightful
silhouettes they made. All at once, in the penumbra, I was surprised by Colling's hand in the shape of an inverted cone with the
fingers squeezed together as if he were about to sprinkle something; then the cone turned over and the fingertips were raised to
the mouth and the explanation was that from within the cone jut-
ted a very white cigarette that became visible when he pursed his
upper lip to put it in his mouth. His way of lighting a match had to
be seen. At the first gulp of smoke, he coughed and raised his hand
to his mouth. I already knew by heart what that hand looked like as
it intercepted the cough, how thick the black lines at the ends of
his fingernails were; the sight of it was full of immense charm, and
there was a charm, too, in remembering the afternoons when the
sun shone into that parlor and the mysterious atmosphere those
two created there; the brilliant light had an alchemy, a vitality that
would later make me think it was all unreal, like a lie that had once
been true in a dream. And the farther the sun descended the more
surprising the muffled shapes became, not only reminding me of

the forms that had been visible until a moment ago, but also suggesting the color and meaning of the objects now slowly blanketed in shadow.

With the arrogance of one who possesses what another does not, I thought of the pleasure of lying in bed in the dark, a stream of light falling from the green shade of a table lamp onto a book you are reading which is making you imagine color: a scene in the tropics with lots of sunlight, all the sunlight imaginable, shining on mountains and all the varying greens of the jungle. I thought up a whole orgy and lechery of sight, first in a vulgar quest for quantity and then with a perverse refinement of quality: from close or distant visions, blindingly illuminated, of landscapes with sands and seas and wild beasts and men in raging battle, to the artifices of cinema—two airplanes crashing into each other in one of those brief glimpses that seem fleeting to the spectator but have cost the movie studio much time and fabulous sums of money. Then came the sight of microbes swarming in the full moon of a lens, and after all that, every form of art that we take in through the eyes, and even those times when art penetrates terrible shadows and is wondrous for the sole fact of being seen.

At night, before falling asleep, I imagined the tragedy of the blind, but—and this struck me as very odd—I could not imagine their tragedy without visual imagery.

Colling had spoken to blind Elnene, blind Elnene to his family, someone in his family to the long-lived ladies, the long-lived ladies to my mother, my mother to my father, the two of them to me, and Colling was going to come and give me lessons in harmony; he would be paid one peso per lesson, in light of the fact that, etc., etc. At that time we were living in a house on the upper end of Calle Minas. One afternoon, Colling arrived with his guide or *lazarillo* whose name was Fito. Colling held out his soft hand; and there as ever were his smile and his conversation, artless but unpredictable. The cigarette, the cough, the hand, the nails, the brown spots beneath the nose, the almost Egyptian posture with the head leaning to one side and the arm crooked upwards on the other, holding the cigarette, the ear that lay flat against the head, but was elongated, with a lobe as wide as the rest of the ear and longer than other people's earlobes. His ears were very similar to a kind of fried cakes they used to make at my house called *lentejuelas* or sequins. He was of average height or less, his face only a bit longer than it was round. I never really knew what shape his head was because its shape changed depending on where you saw it from; it might be a normal size, or broader in back, or round, or it might be the head of a diplomat, or a traveling salesman, or a teacher of harmony, or it was Colling's head, or it might be another head that was not Colling's. Oh, and I was forgetting one of the hands, the one that didn't hold the cigarette, or more specifically the one that responded when he coughed: when he was sitting down he left it resting on his thigh, palm up.

The first harmony lesson was brief but insanely interesting to me. He taught the lesson, played a piece on the piano, and told a story. The lesson was conducted by a method of his own devising. The piece he played, generally by a Frenchman—Widor, Saint-Saëns, Lack, etc.—was more or less pleasant and superficial, but rarely structured in its rhythmical form, or at least not the way he played it. He played all the parts as if he were taking me through a house that was for rent: here's the living room, the dining room, the kitchen, etc. He made the piece not vulgar—however tasteless a work it was—but rhythmical, and the sequence of his performance would present and develop an idea from the compositional perspective. It was as if he were saying, "First this way, then this way, then this way. Good, now we've eaten for today." It isn't that he was at all mechanical; he was a connoisseur, accustomed to an unusual degree of organization, neither unfair nor cold nor very enthusiastic. Quite similar to certain literary critics. He intrigued me greatly and I thought I would never be able to understand his strangeness.

The story was uncomplicated and almost always had to do with his adolescence, when he was a student at a Catholic boarding school for the blind in Paris. There was a boy in his class who had tattled on him—about what I don't know. And Colling said to himself, "I will teach you to be a trai*tor*." So he asked "ze trai*tor*" to switch desks with him; Colling went to ze trai*tor*'s place and ze trai*tor* to Colling's. When the brother—that was what they called the priest who taught them, who was blind, too—asked Colling a question about the lesson, Colling didn't answer. After much calling upon and asking without being answered by Colling, the brother grew furious and went over to Colling's desk but dealt a tremendous slap to ze trai*tor*.

As he told the story, he laughed wildly. (The cough, the hand, the nails.)

Before he left, I would give him the peso. He smoothed it out, folded it very symmetrically in two, then in four, and in eight, placed it in one of the upper pockets of his jacket; then took out another peso, folded up the same way, from his pants pocket, and put that one in the other top pocket of his jacket. All in absolute silence. Since he always combined them differently, I could never figure out the explanation for his way of carrying pesos. Then he held out his soft, warm, sticky hand and gave his smile. I was very fond of him. As soon as he left, Petrona would come in, spurting with laughter, to clean the shreds of tobacco off the piano keyboard with eau de cologne and open the windows. To tell the truth, I didn't pay as much attention to Colling's grubbiness—or to other received ideas—as many people did. I wasn't continually noticing it, or I would quickly forget it; for me it was something about him, something that affected him, which I didn't relate very closely to other people or to social conventions. It was a strange thing, true, but a thing that was specifically his and had to do with his history, and there was no need for us to intervene in any very rigorous way, or bring to bear the same concepts we would bring to bear on other people. My impression of it was quite vague, and I was irritated by the way other people made so much of it. Perhaps this was because I took a dim view of the criticisms they made of him at home: they paid too much attention to certain things because they didn't feel other things as deeply as I did. And there were some things that were true but which I always reacted against nevertheless, because their truth had initially been overemphasized.

One afternoon I came home and found Colling sitting in the dining room with Petrona, who was showing him a blue rag, then a green one, then a red one. It turned out that Colling saw colors. He was sitting in a patch of bright light, and with considerable effort he would name the colors after a long pause. What was more, he carried out his investigation of color with a single eye, since he was not only blind but one-eyed: the other eye had been removed in an operation intended to restore his eyesight. Now, as he tried to make out the colors, he laboriously swiveled his one eye which dragged a yellowy, pinkish cloud and a lot of tiny red threads behind it. Consequently, we, in our turn, perceived that his lone eye was blue. He never failed to hit on the color he was shown, but he couldn't be put to the test very many times because his eye grew tired. From time to time he took out a handkerchief to wipe the eyelid that lay over the hollow space where the other eye had lived. He began losing his sight at the age of five and by eleven had been left as he was now. A long time later, he told us that another operation had recently been proposed to him, with a greater chance of success, but he wasn't interested. When Petrona asked why he didn't want to do it, he answered, "To see wo*men* as ugh*ly* as you *are*? I'm better off as I am."

He wasn't particularly nice to her, but she hadn't given him much reason to be. The first few times he was invited to lunch he was served wine, but we weren't in the habit of drinking it every day, and so one day there was none. He asked for some, and we sent for it. Another time when there was no wine and he asked for some, Petrona passed him a glass of water, telling him it was wine. He drank it without saying a word and Petrona started in with her laughter. On other occasions, when there was no wine and he asked for some and Petrona brought him a glass of water, he first dipped his index finger in the glass, then sucked it.

Colling wanted us to believe that he had twice been on the verge of getting married but only a day or a few hours before the wedding the bride had died on him: once from illness and the other time because of an accident. Petrona unleashed all her laughter and set about unmasking his lies. Once Colling was telling us about a nun who had a "mous*tache*." Petrona asked him, "And how did you know, maestro?" And he: "Because I touched eet."

On the third try he did succeed in getting married. But he'd left his wife and two small children in Paris to go on a concert tour. An impresario left him stranded in Buenos Aires. Then he came to Montevideo.

His father "was very distinguished, a great gentleman." His mother, "a vulgar woman, a laundress." And immediately he added, "I take after my father."

I didn't want to ponder my illusions about Colling, nor would I have wanted to realize that they were undergoing certain vicissitudes. During moments like the time he spoke disparagingly of his mother, other things I would rather not have remembered came to mind. Generally, when one of these vicissitudes occurred, I managed to suspend the judgment or notion that immediately began to form; I didn't allow this latest reason for questioning my illusions to gain any ground, but said to myself—thinking of him—"poor man!" and prepared to justify or forget the event in question. And then, though his words or gestures remained in memory, this intention gradually extinguished or transformed them, and that first negative thought which had so quickly arrived at the site of the incident—and threatened to remain attached to what would then become a bad memory or even to increase its ill will—would gradually vanish.

The negative thought was like a tiny figure trying to reach an island, but my illusions quickly flooded the island in order to drown the thought. And no sooner did I find myself with an island on my hands, then I'd already made the figure who was trying to reach that island disappear. But when Colling spoke disdainfully of his mother, the figure made an unexpected and desperate try for life. At those moments I looked at Colling and all his features, his whole person, even his clothes, wore a different expression. What I thought of him—of the mystery of his knowledge and the strangeness of his life—also took on a different meaning, as if the light on a landscape had momentarily changed. That time, however—beyond the naïve pride I took in not only forgiving him but finding him charming—the weight of bitter reality was too great, and he was not only unjustified but losing his originality. It was then, too, that one memory led to others—and the figure with the island was saved and had already summoned up other thoughts. Now Colling's filthiness no longer seemed so original; now it was related to society. I thought that although my family had overreacted by taking certain things too much into account, I had overreacted by not taking them into account at all. But something else was going on, as well. In some sense, I had in fact taken those things into account, and had transformed them into the object of my illusions. That first afternoon when I went to meet Colling and clung, as darkness fell, to the still recent memory of the color the sun had given to the objects in the room, I, too, though I didn't know it, had arrived there with colors and shadows of my own, which tended to be inflected with meanings that were quite predetermined and also quite accidental. I had illuminated Colling's landscape in a way that even made use of its defects in order to put them in a penumbra—thus giving them value as the objects of a suggestive penumbra—and as they went in secret to join with the as yet unknown whole, they bore traces that mysteriously signified the foreseen totality.

But when Colling projected a beam of harsh, vulgar, wounding light, I discovered that not all his tints were so beautifully aesthetic or apt to blend together when summoned by that mysterious totality, but that they came apart, lost their value, and shamefully disintegrated, revealing shapes like random assortments of junk, the kind of inexpressive shapes that clutter up landscapes and that painters omit.

That was more than twenty years ago. Now, as I breathe over these memories, I'm sitting on a red stool with my elbows on a little blue table, surrounded by the green and gold glints of sunlight on plants, in an open shed with a dirt floor which belongs to a house that is always deserted at this hour. As I live through these memories in this present time, each morning has an unforeseeable way of being unique. Yet what is most unique—the spirit in which I live each morning, my particular way of experiencing it, the variations in the sunlight that falls onto things, the shapes of the clouds that move past or hover in place—all of that, I forget. The only things left are the objects around me, which I know are the same. Every night before I go to sleep I'm curious to know not only what the following morning will be like, but also how I will see my memories in the morning, and what those memories will be like. Sometimes I concentrate on them so hard that the present moment startles me. And it isn't specifically the morning of this day—when everything was so enjoyable and I took pleasure in living, feeling secluded and stealing time from my sorrows—but the times in which I now live that are becoming incomprehensible to me. I've renounced the difficult feat of knowing what I was like in those days or what I am like now, and in what ways I was better or worse then than I am now. Sometimes I think about how long and tolerant life is, after having squandered so much of it. At other times, when I think of my friends who have died while I'm still alive, I feel that my time is stolen and I must live it furtively. Or I imagine that I've taken it upon myself to write these memories at the behest of someone inside me, someone who knows more than I do and wants me to write them down because I'll soon be going to my death from some unknown illness. And then I can feel how the members of my family will live on after my death, remembering me tenderly. And no more? But no, there will be more: I throw myself voraciously onto the past while thinking of the future and the form these memories will take. That's why I see them so differently each day. And that form will be the only thing that remains to me of the unique feeling of each day. The effort I make to grasp these memories and launch them into the future will hold me suspended in the air while death crosses the earth. As I rummage through my memories every morning, I don't even know if it is really my memories that I'm flailing around in, or why. Or how it can be that I'm rummaging or flailing around in my own life, even though I'm speaking of other people. And while I'm rummaging in the mornings, I don't know what's happened during the night, what secrets have joined forces without my knowledge, just before sleep came, or beneath it.

I've stirred up my memories many times. At first they surprised me, not only by making me relive some strange past event, but also because the different persona that is mine these days conceives them in a new way. And without intending to, I must have remembered them many times in different shapes than those I now imagine; I must have covered them in concepts, like veils or substances, that modified them; I must have moved them around and altered my first glance, I must have seen some things in a different order than before. I don't know which memories have faded or disappeared, but many of those that reach my consciousness are forced to become concrete and clear. Some must have deceived me with their audacity or grace or new charms—and some must have been replaced by things that have happened to other people, things I've been especially drawn to and have taken for my own. But now I've merged all the different phases and the things I've added to them into one, and I would go so far as to stake my head on it, with the most absolute certainty and good faith: I would wager myself to be the author of a new certainty, a certainty that would be willing, in all innocence and without irony, to bet on its own truth. Was I ever really that teenager who   was perpetually and intimately timid with Colling, or did I ride in roughshod in the way of teenagers, hastily presuming to be on familiar terms with the unknowable? Did my early attempts to comprehend him—when I went so quickly from one feeling to another and Colling's nuances blended together or shamefully scattered in all directions—actually increase my fondness for him, even though I thought less of him? What new things did he present me with—even as I invented them—so that I could start afresh? Or was it simply that I didn't feel like losing my illusions, after all I had put into them, like a businessman who finds himself involved in a bad deal and risks and invests even more in order to save himself? Or what was happening? And what other things were happening?

But let's go back to concrete facts, facts that have taken each other as witnesses and formed an association among themselves to certify their legitimacy—although no one knows exactly when they should have taken out a patent as new inventions.

One afternoon, almost at dusk, I was walking along Calle 18, and there in the café that used to be near Calle Yi was Colling. It had been a long time since I'd seen him. He was with his *lazarillo*. In front of him was a large glass, full of a milky drink. He began telling me about absinthe, explaining how it was prepared: a small amount in a large glass, and then water poured in, drop by drop.

And then it was called pernod. It was his drink.

Around that time, some society people had organized a committee to protect him. No doubt they were Catholics who had admired him at the church of Los Vascos and were pained by the state he was living in. He had a following among the priests of that church, to whom he had introduced me. Since that was a period when I was mostly "living on the moon," I didn't know why the committee had been organized, I'd only heard the rumor that flew across Montevideo: "Colling took a bath, Colling took a bath." And I'd heard that this committee was organizing a series of concerts he would give at the Evangelical Temple on Calle Constituyente. (It occurs to me now that there couldn't have been much of a relationship between the people from Los Vascos and those of the Evangelical Temple. But perhaps they simply requested the temple as a venue because it had a large organ and the hall was suitable for concerts.)

He played certain pieces very fast. I can't remember who it was that used to say he played so quickly in order to show that he could play as fast as a sighted person or faster. He may also have played some works fast because they struck him as bland or boring, from the perspective of his knowledge of harmony; or because he'd played them so often that they no longer offered him any of the pleasure a pianist feels when he plays something new, something different from the pieces he's already mastered; or he may have played them quickly because he didn't remember them very well— the tendency in that case is to speed up the performance, "to get past the dangers fast." But the truth is that he did play some pieces too fast, which gave rise to a lamentable public incident. When the great Argentine pianist Ernesto Drangosh was in Montevideo, at a gathering attended by all of society, he listened to Colling play a prelude and fugue for organ by Bach. When everyone went over to congratulate Colling afterwards and he was surrounded by very serious people, Drangosh, after paying his compliments, told him quietly that he had recently been in Germany and they played the fugue more slowly there. And Colling answered, "Ah! Zhat's because zhe Germans' backsides weigh zhem down more zhan a French*man*'s does!"

That afternoon Colling told me that when the committee instructed him not to drink absinthe he answered that he was the master of his own acts and sent the committee packing.

We left the café on foot and I went back with them to the tenement on Olimar between Calle 18 and Colonia where they were living. As we were concluding our conversation, people skirted past us on their way into the tenement. It had already been dark for a while. The angular shadows moving in the center of the narrow entry hall were the most concrete thing for the eyes to settle on as we talked. The shadows advanced and receded as gusts of wind rocked a lightbulb that dangled over the middle of the street. There was nothing else there but old, dirty, dingy shapes, a smell, and the arrival and departure of unfamiliar people, etc.

I never knew exactly which room belonged to Colling and the family that moved with him from tenement to tenement, a couple with many sons. Once they were of school age the sons—during the hours they weren't in school—would become Colling's *lazarillos*, and then, after that, paper boys. The education they received in school struck Colling as inadequate, and he would teach them history on his own. When I arrived at the café, he was talking to the boy about history; they were finishing up with Napoleon.

I hadn't been able to find out which room was Colling's, though several times, at different hours of the day, I had gone as far as the tenement's entrance. Though at night that crowded building clamped its dirty, crumbling black jaws down on the entryway, which responded to the lightbulb that swung in the middle of the street by muttering shadows against its light, by day a bright courtyard was visible down the hall, open to the sky, with sunlight shining on laundry hung out to dry (white, pink, red, salmon, black, etc.—and once I saw some immense lilac-colored pillowcases billowing in the wind). The courtyard was paved with large stones, varnished with grime, and the shadows of the clothes hanging on the line moved across little puddles of soapy water. There were other shadows, too, that appeared in turns: sometimes they lay in front of the rooms on the right and at other times next to the rooms on the left. At the back of the entrance hall, on the right side, Colling would appear with his *lazarillo* when I least expected them.

A long time later—I don't know how much time or what things had happened over the course of it—I went to fetch Colling one morning because his *lazarillo* couldn't accompany him that day. He was living in a different tenement, and we had moved, as well, to another house on Calle Minas. That morning I hadn't wanted to leave the house, though two days earlier I'd been anxiously waiting for the moment to go for Colling because I had finished a composition and was very eager for him to hear it. But now I was fed up with it: my exalted conception of it and my illusions, which only a little while before had risen so high, had collapsed. Because now I was working on something else: I had begun to unleash my fury on behalf of—or against—Schumann's *Carnival*. I'd started in on it the day before and it was consuming all my energies; my whole spirit was filled with its beauty and with the abyss of promises it made me as I imagined all the pleasure that would be mine once I'd learned it. All of that, multiplying and taking on new forms, was now heightening the immediate, uncontrollable pleasure of hurling myself upon it almost brutally. The night before I had been churning my hands, my head and my whole soul about in the *Carnival* until very late. And before I fell asleep I'd sworn to get up early so I would have time to keep at it until the moment came to go out for Colling. But I tended to remain in any state of inertia for far too long, and getting up that morning was particularly difficult.

It was a limpid, luminous morning and I woke up very close to it, for my room was a long attic with a low skylight looking directly up into the morning sky. When I awoke, I thought about the *Carnival* and sensed the day; it was the kind of day that makes someone in the family say what a lovely day it is, and that it would be lovely to go to this or that place, and the voices you heard had a special sonority and you stayed still, listening to them. And then you're in the mood to get up slowly, and you reward yourself for having accomplished that task by lighting a cigarette. The bright sunshine makes you wrinkle up your face in defense of your eyes. As you squint, your mouth stretches out as if you were smiling. And at that point you might as well smile. Since the morning is lovely and someone tells a joke and this is the day, the hour and the opportunity to reconcile yourself with something, you keep the smile, which is only interrupted when your lips pucker around the tube of bitter *mate*. And that's how the time went by, until I had to hurry out to get Colling without having gotten my hands on the *Carnival* at all.

We were living on Minas between Asunción and Lima. The sidewalk was lined with old paradise trees. I walked along Minas towards Calle 18. The sunlight broke everything into pieces and even seemed to be fragmenting the sounds of the day. The morning was miraculous. My attention floated over everything, and I had to concentrate on keeping up a quick pace. Even the dust that rose between the horses' legs and the spokes of a heavy wagon's wheels was distracting. I kept having to quicken my steps once more. Some time later, when I'd finally managed to adjust to my new momentum, I was able to go quickly and without stopping to Colling's place. I'd found out from him that his latest tenement was on Calle Gaboto, near the sea; it was the first time I'd gone there. This tenement was a little less dirty and crowded than the last one, but the arrangement of the rooms was fairly similar. There were washbasins in the middle of the courtyard, and a woman was doing some laundry at one of them.

"Does Colling, the maestro, live here?"

"No maestro lives here."

"You haven't seen him pass by with a *lazarillo*?"

"A *lazarillo*? What do you eat that with?"

"That's the kid who goes around with a blind man."

"Oh, the blind man. That room there, second from the rear."

I tapped lightly with my knuckles. The woman shouted "Go on in," in a voice and with a gesture that seemed to be a synthesis of, "oh *leave off* with your formalities and just *go in*; you've already tried to bamboozle me with your *lazarillo*." What a pity! She was young and pretty, but nothing friendly emerged from beneath the big white kerchief tied around her head.

I pushed the door and oof! . . . Colling's awful miasma washed over me. Even so, I went in. But I couldn't bring myself to shut the door behind me. Two steps away from me were his feet in the bed; the headboard stood against the wall. As I was adjusting to the darkness and waiting for Colling to wake up, I gradually made out the objects in the room. I had already said "maestro," but not very loudly, and he hadn't answered. Since he was blind, I couldn't tell whether he was awake or not. The room was small and full of derelict objects: parts of a sideboard, chairs with busted caning and missing legs, and other pieces of cast-off furniture. In the corner to the left was a small wardrobe made of white wood that was blackened by dirt; it seemed one-eyed like its owner because it had a bit of mirror on one side only. And—perhaps just as I was thinking that Colling couldn't look at himself in that mirror—he woke up. He said, "Aha!" like someone finding something he was expecting to find. And a series of occurrences began that were strange to me. First he said it was early; then he started pushing away a pinkish blanket, and there on his neck were his collar and a bow tie of the sort that clips on, then his vest, and finally a hand which went to the vest pocket, took out his watch—a gift that someone, I don't know who, gave to those blinded during the great war—touched the dial with its raised dots, then closed the lid and put it away. The other hand—all of this while he was still lying in bed—went to the drawer of the bedside table—made of the same white wood as the little one-eyed wardrobe—and took out cigarettes and matches. As he blew smoke out past the stains under his nose and coughed, the hand that took out the watch—the one I was used to expecting melodic surprises from—reached beneath the bed and took out a bucket made from a kerosene can. Into it, he spat. But the great surprise was when suddenly he threw the pinkish—I say pinkish only to give its color a name—blanket off entirely and stood up beside the bed. I thought—also with surprise—of a medieval page boy in a Dumas novel. Past the bottom of the vest flowed the shirt, bunched up like a short, puffy skirt or a meringue, and covered with faded stains of the type usually seen on antique maps of the world. Below was the whole naked body, very white. The sudden nakedness is what must have made me think of a page boy's close-fitting leggings. And his hovel of a room   must   have reminded me of the atmosphere of a Dumas novel. At the nether extreme of his person—I had begun my scrutiny from the head—were the socks, folded down over his boots. These were actually quite shiny, undoubtedly because he had tossed and turned while he slept.

He put his pants on, then knocked on a door to my left and the mother of the *lazarillos* came in. He introduced her to me. She was friendly and smiling. And just at that moment I looked at the blanket and saw some bugs moving across it—I don't know if they were fleas or bedbugs. Then I raised my gaze to meet the living eye of the one-eyed wardrobe. I hadn't made a move, but I thought of how my mother and sisters would have squealed if they'd seen that. The lady left and came back with a washbowl. When she had gone and closed the door, Colling told me with a smile, "She

brings me '*ot* wat*er* today because zhou are here." He picked up
the towel from the back of a chair and dipped one corner of it into
the washbowl, which was on the seat of the chair. He swiped the
wet corner behind his ears, across his forehead and over the hollow
where his other eye had once lived, and then put the towel back on
the chair. I no longer wondered about the two marks under his
nose or the cracked layer of grime on the rest of his head.

I wanted to leave that room as soon as I could, but he said there
was no rush and told me all about the father of the *lazarillos* who
came home very late every night, drunk and shouting for his wife.

We went out into the morning very contentedly and he began
telling me an anecdote about something that once happened to him
with Saint-Saëns. I'd already heard about it, though in less detail,
from a Uruguayan family who had heard the story in Paris. Which
meant that there was some possibility it was true. Colling described the Parisian drawing room where this curious encounter
had taken place. Thinking about the wretched hovel we had just
left in contrast to the Parisian drawing room, I suddenly remembered the bugs and realized that since I'd given Colling my arm
they might be running over onto me. Although the idea afflicted
me greatly I tried to ignore it; the morning was so lovely that
worrying about that now, as we were walking along so happily and
he was telling me such an interesting anecdote, seemed a pettiness
and a betrayal.

The two of them, Colling and Saint-Saëns, had been invited to
that Parisian drawing room as if to a duel, for it seems that someone had gone to Saint-Saëns "with the story" that Colling was
a great improviser. On the field of honor, Saint-Saëns said to
Colling: "They tell me you are doing extraordinary things, despite
your youth. And that reminds me of my own youth, for in those
days I did unusual things, too." Here Colling told me in an aside
that Saint-Saëns was very proud. And I, who knew how proud
Colling was, remembered a cartoon I once saw, I'm not sure where,

of two terrible liars shaking each other's hands: its caption read, "Two great powers greet one another." And indeed Colling answered him, "All right, let's see if ze zhings I'm doing now, while I am young, can be compared with ze zhings you are doing now zhat you are not so young." To which the other man replied, "Fine, then I shall improvise first." They improvised in the styles of Palestrina, Bach, Beethoven, Schumann, Schubert, Chopin, Wagner, and Liszt. The musicians in attendance drew lots to see who would furnish the themes. Saint-Saëns began with the style of Palestrina. The more antique the composer, the more difficult it is to improvise in his style, because one is restricted to the limited techniques and very rigid rules of that composer's era; the improviser naturally tends to make use of the expanded techniques and liberties of today. At the first chord, Colling placed his hand on Saint-Saëns' shoulder and asked, "Is that chord part of the improvisation?" When Saint-Saëns, very annoyed, told him it was and that Palestrina used that chord, Colling answered, "Yes, but never to begin; Palestrina used that chord only under certain circumstances and in relation to a certain other chord, and in no case at the beginning of a composition." After that it got even worse; Colling interrupted him all the time and at last it was decided that Colling would have to contain himself until the end. According to Colling, Saint-Saëns had improvised everything more or less badly, Wagner worst of all. (Colling described himself as "a fanatical admirer of Wagner.") Saint-Saëns' best improvisation was Liszt, said Colling. Then Colling improvised, without a single interruption from Saint-Saëns, who said, at the end, "This young man has beaten me, but he's the only one." Colling told me the story with that ending. And he added that afterwards they'd become very good friends and Saint-Saëns had invited him to visit an estate he had in Algeria.

Almost this whole while I was watching the ground so Colling

wouldn't stumble. I remembered that he had complained that
Héctor—his last *lazarillo*—didn't warn him when he stepped off
or onto a curb or about any other obstacle, so that he walked along
stumbling and almost falling. I had listened to Colling's anecdote
with some difficulty, my level of attention uneven and somehow
fragmented. This wasn't because he would break off, or because I
was more attracted, at that point, by the sights and sounds of the
morning, or because I had to be constantly on the alert to keep
Colling from stumbling. Rather I would say that it was my attention that was stumbling, and it was stumbling against inconvenient
thoughts, certain anxieties and impediments I always had on hand
in order to render myself incapable of being happy just at the moment when I could have been. Suddenly, while Colling was talking,
I would realize that I had fallen behind his story and was running
after his words, tripping and trying to catch up. Then I had to resort to the immediate recollection of his words which weren't fully
recorded yet and hadn't begun to become memories. And it irritated me to have to pursue this trail of fresh tracks, just beginning
to sink in to my memory; I felt ridiculous, clutching at an echo and
hurriedly scanning its contents. If Colling's anecdote was like a
carpet being rolled out as we walked, and my eye was drawn to its
weave, design, and color, then you might say that there were other
things that drew my eye as well—something like lumps moving
around under the carpet. I saw the lumps and their movements,
but didn't know what objects were making them. So, to conjure
away my anxiety, I had to raise the carpet and uncover the objects,
but then I didn't have time to watch the movement of those anxieties because I had to run along behind Colling's words. Only
when his conversation slackened or was of little interest did the
anxieties seize the chance to enter my mind; they blocked out the
living instants and demanded that I attend to them instead. Some
of them were already on the prowl; they were connected to the girl
with the kerchief on her head. Wasn't it true that because she was

pretty I had wanted to make myself impressive by saying a refined word? For her, *lazarillo* would be a refined word. And hadn't I grown anxious because I sensed a reaction to my posturing in the attitude with which she answered? The same thing was always happening to me with certain of my own actions. They came unexpectedly, took me by surprise, and woke me up; I acted spontaneously and happily, never knowing or imagining that my actions would later come back to haunt me. Nor did I know which ones would come back and be stuck to me forever by anguish. When the girl reacted to me like that, I was left contemplating her: I was completely taken up with contemplating her and even obeying her, for example, when she told me to go in. Then my own passive stance stayed in my memory, shaming me, and I was irritated with myself to the point of anguish. At times I succeeded—even me— in reacting at the right moment. But my accursed rhythm, my slowness, ensured that I almost always came too late or out of place. And those would be the actions that would come back to me. Even years later they might come back. And when I remembered them, inevitably, all my muscles would suddenly contract.

Another thing that came back to me that morning was Colling's bugs. After my initial surprise and the thought of the brouhaha my family would have raised if they'd seen them, I realized the bugs really hadn't made as big an impression on me as they should have, and that in order to feel great repugnance I would have had to spend some time meditating on the ignominy of those bugs. Then I began to wonder whether I wasn't lacking in sensitivity, or whether my disgust was based on received ideas, and then came a whole series of other thoughts, of the kind that barely even manage to become thoughts.

When Colling spoke the name of Schumann during his anecdote, I'd remembered the *Carnival* and was assailed by a desire to hurl myself upon it and by the anguish of not being able to. That day, my urge had many opponents: people, events, circumstances—and the harmony lesson would be the worst of them, not only because each lesson was more complicated and painful than the last, but also because I would have to spend time on my composition, which I was disenchanted with. And instead of thinking of something else, I went on thinking about that: I suddenly felt the need to attend to the obstacles that emerged in my path, as if I had developed a passion for collecting them—perhaps because I was somehow justifying a tendency that was taking on the proportions of a real misfortune. My way of protesting against these opponents was to demonstrate to them the harm their opposition was doing me. But that didn't matter to my opponents, and I was the one who came out the loser, for once this feeling of distress started up I couldn't stop it. And my sensitivity grew even keener and more delicate and brought me fresh anguish. Therefore I felt ridiculous and unfortunate, running along behind Colling's words to catch their echo, then suddenly stepping on their heels, stopping, thinking of my urge and the anguish that dully persisted like those lumps slowly moving under the carpet, and then running along behind Colling again and thinking once more of the actions that were stuck to me now like the legs and wings of swamp insects.

During the siesta hour, my sister, the oldest one, read him the political articles that appeared in the magazine *Atlántida*. If this had happened when I was first becoming acquainted with him, I would have felt obliged—by some momentary weakness—to stay with him during the reading, even though the articles didn't interest me and it would always cost me some effort to enter into the reading and then even more effort to emerge. But now we were on close enough terms that we didn't feel obliged to do the same thing if it wasn't of interest to both of us. So I stretched out on my bed. From there I could hear Colling's cough and I began to think about his life. He didn't appear to be concerned by it: he was wearing an old life and it was very comfortable. Of course his old life was in-fested with bugs and that couldn't always be comfortable; I re-membered that a few times during our lessons, no doubt when he couldn't stand the itching any longer, he would suddenly let loose with a slap—with the startling violence of a sprung mousetrap—and embark on a long, mad bout of scratching. Now I was trying to imagine how Colling had reached that state of unconcern. Perhaps if he had been told that someone—one of his admirers—would go to his room and kill all the bugs, so that when he got home not one would be left, he would have answered, "good"—as he did when I suggested the correct way of resolving some harmonic chords. But if killing the bugs were to imply any sort of immediate incon-venience or trouble; if, as we left the house, I were to tell him to wait a moment, that we were going to send to the pharmacy for some insecticide powders, then he would have refused the offer: "No, in zhat case, no; I can go on as I have."

He must be lazy even in his pleasure; to keep from having to go looking for it in inaccessible places, he would force his pleasure to crawl into whatever corners first presented themselves; in this case, his pleasure could make do with the immediate fact of scratching himself.

The sadness Colling's abandonment inspired in me took on a variety of colors; when I thought he was apathetic by nature, the sadness took on a certain touch of humor; it was a sad little joke. But if I thought he was like that because of the incomprehension of those around him, then I felt implicated in some way and the sadness was mingled with a certain vexation that doesn't lend itself to pleasant descriptions. Perhaps, in order to be profoundly sad for someone, I would have needed, among many other things, an ex-cellent imagination. I barely managed to come up with an impres-sion that Colling hadn't always been like that, or at least not to that extreme, and that of all the things he had set in motion in his life what had picked up the greatest force and preserved the greatest momentum was harmony, while all the rest must have gradually died off. Earlier, his pride in being a great musician probably extended to all the other parts in his life, and his conduct must have evinced greater unity or connection; wedded to his youthful pride had probably been the desire to display an attitude and style of life with as much aesthetic dignity as he found in his art. Then the tendency to let himself go must gradually have grown more pronounced, the tendency to show less and less concern for anything that wasn't music, and to justify his abandonment with the fatalistic ideas that are now so habitual in so many minds. And then the notion that he couldn't be concerned about himself—in the sense of cleanliness—must have been waiting for him with open arms, because "he had other concerns," and because "everything is forgiven an artist." But—when I knew him, at least—Colling justified his grubbiness differently: "Others are to blame; zhey abandoned me." Once, in a café, he said to me, "Under zhis French"—*fránces*, he pronounced it—"good humour of mine, I have such a pessim*ism*!" At the time, his way of speaking struck me as vulgar posturing. Since then I've met with other avowals expressed just as feebly or clumsily, which initially made me indignant over their appearance of falsity, or were so comically absurd it took a great effort not to laugh. For the person in possession of a sorrow does not always have at hand the expression that we know to be the appropriate one. What pained me most was not that a sorrow was being concealed, but that the person suffering from it could give the terrible impression of having put on the wrong mask. And Colling had thrown me off many times. Already, taking together his great virtues and his lack of hygiene, I had developed a tendency to want to discover, in the mystery of other famous men, little hygiene where I saw great virtues. And in fact, sometimes that was not the case.

When we sat together in the parlor that afternoon, I'd had time to play the *Carnival* a little while earlier. Nevertheless, he proposed—either for the chance to address an important work or because he perceived my enthusiasm—that I analyze certain parts of it. I remember I also played my own composition, the one I'd grown sick of and abandoned in favor of my newly awoken enthusiasm for the *Carnival*, and it now seemed better to me. At that point, Colling, wanting to make some corrections, sat down at the piano and played a few passages of my composition from memory, and I began thinking about his memory. My ideas and feelings about his work and his life, which had so many consequences, must have taken shape from there. I don't know if it was that very afternoon or another similar one when I also pondered his memory and he taught me the Chinese modes. Just prior to that he had told me that after hearing a forty-minute symphony twice he remembered it so clearly that he was later able to transcribe the whole thing for piano. Then he began teaching me the Chinese modes. Once long ago he had composed a piece that made use of them: it was titled *Manchuriana*. He told me that the Chinese modes had a celestial quality, and therefore he'd used them to describe a wedding in Manchuria, or had invented a wedding to take advantage of the Chinese modes. Then, to give the work some "variety" he had come up with a series of chords that were brusque and picturesque, and had interrupted the wedding with them, sending a battalion of Cossacks past during the ceremony. Then the wedding returned, and at the end the battalion echoed in the distance.

I was sad that afternoon. At first, I was as delighted with Colling's composition as a child with a present. But a gradual sadness came over me. And I realized that the sadness was already starting even in my initial delight. It was like the sadness evoked, after the first moment, by certain toys that belong to other children, toys you find quite ugly, but you see that the other child loves them very much. It was also the sadness of a worn-out relic someone else is preserving. Colling had placed these dolls—the bride and groom at their wedding, the Cossacks—in a glass case, and it was all very far away in his youth and covered with cobwebs. And he didn't know it was cobwebbed and far away; he lived with that time enclosed within him, and because he communicated with us, he believed he was living now. But he lived his present life with that other, earlier time, locked up inside him. Knowing little about each other, we got along very well, but we lived different lives, in different times.

He did have a great memory. But I began paying far less attention to that; it started to seem like a bad habit of his. When people came to hear him play, I'd show off his memory as if I were showing off an old monkey, tired of doing the same trick. But in addition to the bad habit of storing things in his memory, he had a mania for improvising, and in that he was as obstinate as a would-be record-breaker.

Colling was like a train station from which certain vehicles, always more or less the same ones, departed while others arrived, though he would suddenly alter their shapes and it would take me a moment to realize that they were the same ones. At first I thought the vehicles were always different and startlingly novel. And that continued up to a certain point. But then the alterations or changes gradually lost their initial flair; however many different routes they took, the vehicles were starting to look the same and the business was immediately recognizable. Suddenly I was discovering that Colling was more like the administrator who managed a transport business than like the company founder. If he were asked to improvise in the style of a composer—if, for example, he were given four notes to improvise upon in the style of Beethoven—he quickly had the vehicle at the ready: Beethoven. Curiously enough, he also claimed to put himself in the spirit of Beethoven. Listening to him, you encountered something, forms or chords, that had been constant in the life and compositions of Beethoven; it all had a strong flavor of Beethoven. But the improvisation quickly tipped its hand; we found we had been duped in our delight and were vexed by the adulteration. This thing had been made with some residue of Beethoven or some consequences of his work that could be deduced after the fact: it was a wax museum Beethoven, sad to look at. But we could take another vehicle—the real Beethoven. So the falsification was pointless. And when we did take an authentic Beethoven composition, everything changed, as in a dream; Beethoven's music was alive and there was no more vehicle.

But of course, Colling didn't seek to pass off what was his as Beethoven's. The merit lay in the fact that it wasn't Beethoven, but resembled him nonetheless. Colling was a romantic forger who didn't try to pass his bills off as genuine or buy anything with them. He was no speculator in forged bills. On the contrary, his interest lay in showing that this was his, and his ability to do it attested to his knowledge and skill. Dull heads would drink in that skill with great wonder; it would make them think of genius. Those whose admiration began from there would then go on to suppose who knows what, and often ended up deducing something like this: If a man can imitate the works of others in this way, what must his own work be like! But to me, his own work was sad, like a child who loves a vulgar toy and clings to it tenderly.

A long time later it made me much sadder to learn that he had put his furniture in storage and was sleeping at the Salvation Army. One afternoon my sister, the one who recited "Pobre María," told me, "Mama is already convinced, and all we need now is Papa. We'll put him in the little room near the stairway that leads up to your attic." And all our happiness stretched out before us.

One morning his furniture arrived: the little one-eyed wardrobe and bedside table made of white wood, the bed and another small table on which he worked. He would come that evening. All of us had resolved that when he arrived, there would be no one in the house but me. Then I would offer to wash his feet, and there was a chance he would accept. We were all very glad. But I pretended to be sad and told him, "It's hard to believe, maestro,

the way you've been abandoned! To think that you've had to go
and sleep in that place which may even be infested with bugs, who
knows!" And before I'd finished he began answering, "In Paris, I
was a gentle*man*," raising his tone on the final stress of "gentle-
man." When he agreed to put his feet in water, I brought a large
basin and began taking off his shoes. He had on two pairs of socks.
He left the inside pair on all the time because taking them off
would have hurt some sores and boils on his legs. I removed them
very slowly, soaking his feet in the warm water. I still remember
the light of the portable lamp shining on all that. The situation
was so strange that to keep my spirits up my head entertained me
with half-jesting thoughts. When I saw that his toenails had grown
so long they curled into talons, my head started thinking that
Darwin was right: man does descend from the apes.

Though his great faculty for memorizing and improvisation
seemed to have advanced to the point of devouring the greater part
of his mind and soul—or to have emerged from inside him to develop beyond the natural contours of his soul—and though the
value of the stock I placed in his virtues had fallen, the truth was
that he was still an organist, and a masterful one. Despite his
physical state, which at that point did not lend itself to illusions,
the first morning that I woke up to the knowledge that Colling was
in the house, I felt his presence as a nameless prestige. He had
come to our home by an accident, by a not entirely understood
privilege of circumstances. Something in his mystery traveled in-
cognito. And the whole thing was as inoffensive as a book written
in antiquity.

He often got up in the night and rummaged through the one
little drawer in his work table. The sound of his footsteps—he persisted in sleeping with his shoes on—broke in on my light sleep.
But the phases of my sleep weren't thrown off, for my sleep was
trusting; everything stayed nearby and then gathered together to

go on.

The first time I saw him wash his hands, he ran the tap until the sink was full; then he picked up the soap with the tips of his fingers and rubbed it—with the slow deliberation of a man handling a wondrous gem—over both sides of the opposite hand. Next he submerged his two hands slowly until the palms were touching the bottom of the sink and made some movements, equally slow, with his hands stretched out and his fingers together, as if he were moving objects that left him dumbfounded. Then, as slowly as a submarine must move when it emerges on the surface, he began withdrawing them and asked for the towel. Another time, when he was invited to wash his hands before sitting down at the table, he clapped them together as if he were playing the cymbals in a band—and as if he were expecting some fine dust to rise from them—and said, "Zhere is no necessity."

Just once I saw him angry, and that was in fun. The little one-eyed wardrobe was full of bundles of blank paper that were writings to him because they were covered with raised dots. The morning of the playful anger, he was arranging the bundles and said, "This is destitution, in four volumes." But we would laugh so hard we were crying when he began to sing: he would sing out the names of the notes and the semitones, but as he was naming the semitones, he would smuggle in a few other notes. For example, if he were singing the eight notes of the scale—counting the eighth one—he would say, "do - na- tu-ral - and -re - as - well." In fact he'd named only two notes, do and re, but while he said "natural" and "as well" all the others came in. In the middle of a melancholy Chopin nocturne, he would suddenly sing, "and my B flat as well," and it was impossible not to give your soul over entirely to such an innocent form of delight.

At home they said it upset him when anyone failed to compliment his *lazarillo*. At that point, the *lazarillo* was named Héctor and he was eight years old. He was given magazines to look at in the dining room and when there were preserves in syrup for dessert, he was served a dish of them. One afternoon my younger sister called me over to watch the *lazarillo* from a hiding place; after he had eaten the dessert on his plate he went over to the sideboard, stuck his hand into a tureen full of candied sweet potatoes, took out pieces of sweet potato dripping with syrup, and put them on his plate.

When my sisters visited my attic, he always stationed himself at the foot of the stairs to watch them go up. He had immense black eyes that would fill with tears as he laughed at Colling's stories. At his house, they ate a great deal, and drank wine. Once I saw him in quite a state. We were with Colling in the depths of the Evangelical Temple, where long tables were being prepared for a banquet. After Colling had been invited to partake and had refused, and the lady president of the committee had withdrawn, the *lazarillo*, eyes goggling, grabbed Colling's overcoat and shouted in savage desperation, "Make the most of it, make the most of it, maestro!"

Colling drank a great deal, but no one could say they had ever seen him display the least sign of drunkenness. He drank outside the house because Petrona took away his bottles of eau-de-vie. First he would hide them—in the little wardrobe, under the bed, etc. Then Petrona, with her old trick, would replace the eau-de-vie with water, and then his trick would be to bring them in already filled with water.

One morning I thought he was dead. It was noon and he was still in bed. The *lazarillo* was waiting, immobile as the RCA Victor dog listening to his master's voice. When I went to wake him up he was blue and his breathing was inaudible. I couldn't turn him over, either, because the middle of his bed sagged almost to the floor and he slept practically sitting up. After that I asked him not to drink so much because it scared me. And he agreed, very courteously. I also told him that if he bought himself a mattress after his next concert, we would have his bed fixed. He also agreed to bathe and wear underwear. After the bath, he had white hair, and we went to him and took his arm as if in reconciliation after a lengthy falling out. He confessed to me that he was uncomfortable because he had put on some piece of clothing, I don't know which one, with the opening in the back. After that, he said that he was bathing at La Sagrada Familia—the school where he would go to have lunch. And I believe he even went so far as to sleep several nights with his shoes off. But that was his final venture into the world of hygiene.

Whenever I arrived in an unfamiliar country, a feeling of newness would suddenly present itself in certain objects—the shapes of cigarette packs and matchboxes, the color of the streetcars (but not always in the very different spirit of the people)—and in that same way Colling gave a new sense of life to many kinds of objects. I would observe his actions, his emotions, the rhythm of his moments, and they were like ordinary objects, or else they were objects with a surprise. One night when I was going upstairs he was working in dense darkness at the drawer of his table. At each one of the four corners he had a pile of little figures made of matchboxes, and on each little figure was a harmonic equation written out in raised dots. He combined them in ways I could never understand. He told me that chamber music was in one corner, opera in another, music for solo instruments in another, and symphonic music in another. That night he had made such strange combinations that he finally told me, "Know something? Stravinsky, Prokofiev, you, and all the other madmen like you are right." Before that he'd been their great enemy. At other times, he would write on his Braille slate—a complicated thing to explain—and said he was writing novels about *apaches*, which were like the dime novels we called "Tid-Bits," and in that way he helped support his children in Paris. Another time, after I returned from a distant city where I went once a month to see a sweetheart, he told me, "You go out to seek beauty when you have it right here in your own home; if I were a few years younger I'd set things straight for you." He was referring to my older sister, the one who recited "Pobre María," and who read to him. I answered with a smile he didn't see. I must have smiled the same way the last time I saw him, when we were moving again, to the outskirts of the city, and he was going to have to adjust to another house in the center. On the sidewalk, as we were locking up the empty house, he told me some new fact relating to his extreme lack of hygiene. The *lazarillo* laughed and I must have given that smile. Then I left for another distant city. And when I came back a year later I was told he had died in the Pasteur Hospital, as a result of his drinking. In fact, I never knew what caused his death. I was told about it just after dinner. And I remember that as I strolled beneath tall trees I thought—as people generally think in such cases—about how old he must have been when he died: he must have been fifty, because during the year he lived in our house he turned forty-nine. Then I thought about his mystery.

Whenever I was beckoned or made an instinctive movement towards another person whose mystery had signalled to me in some way—a signal unknown to the person himself—I was tempted to follow the trail of that mystery as if I were concealing my presence behind trees, and I felt a tender sense of how small we would be beneath such immense trees. When Colling began living in our house, I found that his mystery was full of signals and trails, but there was no need to follow them: they paraded before my watching mind even as other things also put in an appearance or happened. It was as if, in that night under the trees, I had forgotten the trail and looked at the tree trunks, listening to the wind in the treetops and watching the branches joining and separating beneath the starry sky, and thinking that however much they murmured, the leaves would never say anything to each other. And things of that sort.

When Colling came to stay in our house, the thoughts that were accumulating and forming concepts and causing my feelings of disillusionment didn't take over Colling's whole being; they didn't extend throughout his mystery but neither did they entirely disappear: the concepts and disillusionments were some of the many things that entered into Colling's mystery. Even as its importance dwindled, the mystery needed ideas that were important to enter into it. But those ideas were simply one more thing: objects, events, feelings, ideas, all were elements of the mystery, and at every moment of life that mystery arranged everything in the strangest way. In the strange conjunction of the elements of an instant, an object would come to rest next to an idea—though in all likelihood, neither of the two would have had any relation whatsoever before then, and they would have none afterwards. A still thing would come to rest beside another that was in motion; other things would arrive, depart, interrupt, surprise, be understood or be incomprehensible—or the meeting might break up. Suddenly the mystery would make unexpected movements, and then I thought that the mystery's soul must be a movement that would disguise itself in different things, events, feelings or ideas, but suddenly the movement would disguise itself as a still thing, a strange object whose immobility was surprising. Suddenly it wasn't only objects that had shadows; events did too, and feelings and ideas also had shadows. And you never knew exactly when the shadow would appear or where it would fall. But if I thought the shadow was a sign of the mystery, later I encountered the mystery and its shadow wandering apart, lost, distracted, and indifferent, without any purpose that could rejoin them. And so the mystery of Colling was abandoned. But from that time on the mystery has lived and grown in my memories. And it returns at many moments and in unexpected forms. Now I remember one of the long-lived ladies, the one who went out to pay calls. She had a large hole in one part of her tulle veil, and when she came to our house she arranged the tulle so that the large hole was in front of her mouth. And through it she put the tube to sip her *mate*.

Note:

Every time "Por los tiempos de Clemente Colling" has been published, this letter from Jules Supervielle has accompanied it:

Dear Sir:

What pleasure I've taken in reading you and coming to know a writer who is truly new and achieves beauty and even greatness through "humility before the subject matter."

You achieve originality without seeking it in the least, by a natural inclination towards depth. You have an innate sense of what will one day be classic. Your images are always meaningful, and because they respond to a necessity they are quick to leave their mark on the spirit.

Your narrative contains pages, absolutely admirable pages, that deserve a place in the most exacting anthologies, and I congratulate you with all my heart for having given us this book.

My thanks as well to your friends who have had the honor of publishing these pages.

Yours,
Jules Supervielle

MY FIRST CONCERT
IN MONTEVIDEO

FOR MANY YEARS, I'D HAD TO practice amid the general distress in my home. At first it wasn't presented to me as a debt problem. All they said at home was that my father had enemies, and when the first one appeared—only his name appeared, mixed up in events that ended badly for my father—I thought about taking revenge: first I would practice in order to become *someone* as soon as possible, then I would find a way to bring shame on our enemy. Sitting at the piano, I summoned up all my strength. But aggression against the piano couldn't last long; the momentum was lost all too quickly. I'd been hurled into that momentum like a ball against the ground, but I bounced lower and lower and finally rolled under the piano to hide.

The general distress in my home was like a sickness, but I didn't know if we'd had some predisposition to it and then contracted it from my father's enemies, or if the contagion had come from numbers. My father knew that numbers would always fill him with illusions and then betray him, but he was fond of them nonetheless and walked around all day with them.

Even in the periods when we were most beseiged with distress, we couldn't do without a little bit of happiness. We all waited for the moment when we would gather together and feel it, like invalids preparing to devour a meager, bland meal as if it were ambrosia.

When the doorbell rang during one of those moments our happiness was cut short, but we were strongly predisposed to win it back. My younger brothers went running out to throw the pursuer off the trail, pointing to a corner around which my father had supposedly just disappeared; they were glad to provide this service at dinner time, for they knew how to adjust to their unhappiness even under the most acute circumstances, as if they'd learned to swallow swords.

During the time I was preparing for it, I had hoped for other consequences from my concert. A few days beforehand, all the furniture in my house changed places. The living room ended up where my parents' bedroom had been, and the piano was now where the headboard of the bed had stood the day we all gathered around it because a man was threatening my father.

During the day, I didn't worry too much about our misfortunes; I worked at the piano, nothing else. If the doorbell rang, I didn't answer. At night, I didn't get much sleep though I was very tired.

Occasionally two painter friends of mine would come over. They came in *without ringing the doorbell*, went around the side of the house and came up to the attic where I slept; then we would all go down to the kitchen and play cards. One friend was tall, with a forehead that bulged out like an ostrich egg. The other one raised his upper lip too high when he laughed, revealing small teeth and a wide expanse of gum. Sometimes we spent the whole night talking. That happened once when my parents weren't there and the three of us all went to sleep in the double bed. But on the nights they didn't come I thought about what my concert would bring me. I had no illusions about the money it would earn; I thought of other results—vague but at least possible and manifold. If I managed to excel, I would have many friends who could influence the authorities to help me live in Montevideo with my wife and daughter, who were in an old city far away. I liked to remember the room where they slept. It was in my wife's family's house. I'd slept in that room the night I met my daughter, who was already more than four months old. The moment I first saw her she was crying because she was a little sick, but for an instant she stopped crying and smiled at me. The night was windy, but I heard another sound that seemed more subterranean. My wife explained: In the Spaniards' time, a water tunnel had been dug down below, and on windy days pieces of wood swept along by the current would knock against the tunnel's walls.

While I was practicing, I wasn't supposed to ponder any memory or dwell on anything that rose up from my imagination. If a memory appeared during the day I kept it at bay with the sound of the piano and the movement of my arms and fingers. But at night, after I was in bed, everything was harder. In addition to thoughts about the piano, I was weighed down with thoughts about my home and its general state of decline, along with the memory of my wife and daughter and my own individual shame and despair. Of course I might be on the verge of solving all these problems, but however optimistic I was, the time that had to elapse before the concert finally arrived would contain the unforeseeable anguish of the nights; the nights were like trenches penning me into a dark field across which I was desperately running. Not only did I have to rush to arrive on time at the place I was going—thus forever eluding the tumult of bad thoughts that were in hot pursuit and gaining on me in the darkness—I also had to race to avoid the other dangers prowling around my home. I was never sure to what extent those dangers arose from my family's temperament or from my own inner core. If I stopped running, I might get used to this unhappiness that contained a small amount of happiness, and never emerge from it. My house was like a sea of greenish waters never subject to great wraths. We navigated across it like poor pirates with little heart for seizing any booty.

I was afraid of wallowing in these thoughts for too long, but I tossed and turned in my bed without being able to fall asleep. All at once I felt my heart beating as if it were a cripple jumping up and down on his lone foot. Then I lay on my back and remembered how my wife would walk through the room before going to bed. Remembering her, my eyes turned her around and around until I fell asleep. One night I dreamed about her.

In the dream, she was walking through a vast church. Candlelight glinted on hues of red and gold. Most of the light fell on her white bridal gown with its long train that she bore slowly forward. She was about to be married but she walked alone, clasping one hand in the other. I was a shaggy dog with very shiny black fur, stretched out on the bride's train. She dragged me along proudly and I seemed to be asleep. At the same time, I felt myself moving through a throng of people who were following the bride and the dog. In that peculiar way of mine, I had feelings and ideas similar to my mother's and was trying to get as close as possible to the dog. He was riding along as serenely as if he'd fallen asleep on a beach and were seeing sea foam all around him when he occasionally opened an eye. I had transmitted an idea to the dog and he received it with a smile. It was this: "You're letting yourself be carried along. But your thoughts are elsewhere."

The greatest danger I was exposed to in those days came from myself. But I would suddenly fall into it as if I were departing for another world, though I knew in advance what things were like there: it was a mute world in which no sound rose. Nevertheless, gardens where imagination ran amok, entwining itself wildly around every fact, kept trying to spring up before my eyes.

I had to practice the piano, and I decided to free myself from my imagination like a drunk resolving to give up liquor, but I carried the bottle around with me all day and slept all night with it on my pillow, and the next day I found that my dreams had gone on a binge.

The morning of the day of the concert, after rushing to have the programs approved and stamped so I wouldn't have to pay a fine, I went to the music center. There they told me I shouldn't be so calm: all concert pianists were a little nervous on the day of a recital. The piano was already in the theater. I went to try it out and found that the floor of the stage sloped so much towards the audience that I was sliding to one side as I played. I spoke to the music center and they told me they could fix it with some small wooden blocks. I don't know why I have such a vivid memory of a moment around noon when I was eating lettuce and looking at my brother's arm, which lay next to mine. This was the arm of a man who would give no concert that day and who had no responsibilities, while my arm was not free and who knew how I would look upon it a few hours later. Even so I wanted the event to take place as soon as possible; I was eager for the pleasure of making a display of bold fury in front of a crowd. At home there was no longer any furniture except the table where we were eating. I would have preferred for it to have been taken away, as well; it reminded me of something I'd recently been told. While I was away in an inland city and my brother had gone off to a small village, a tall, heavyset man came to collect on a bill; his rage overflowed, and he took out a knife and chased my father around that table.

That afternoon I went back to rehearse in the theater, but I noticed that the piano was squealing as if loose strings were striking against each other. I called the music center and they told me someone would be there right away. At that very moment the tuner arrived, laughing: he'd left his tuning fork on top of the strings. A few moments later I received a phone call. I would not be able to give the concert if I didn't leave a deposit of one hundred pesos. I went to the corresponding office. It was a municipal regulation, in case there were fines to be paid afterward; if no fine was levied, the money would be returned. In that office was a gentleman I had met through a very significant person in my life. The gentleman turned out to work there; he took me to his boss, invoked the person—who was significant not only to me—and I was exempted from the deposit. I ran back to the theater. Just then my father dropped by—he didn't know if my mother would be able to come to the concert; she'd lost her shoes, but there was some chance they might be inside the night table which, along with all the other furniture, had been taken to the auction house. That was where my father was headed. I went to the dressing room and put on a smoking jacket, given to me a year before when I gave my first concert in an inland city. On that occasion I had been unable to wear it; the jacket was too small for me, and since my friend had sent it the day of the concert there was no time for tailoring. (Later, with what I earned from the ticket sales, I was able to buy a baby carriage for my daughter—whom I hadn't yet seen then—and an overcoat for myself.)

This would be my first concert in Montevideo. A few moments before it began, I peered through a peephole in the wing to see the upper tiers where those waiting for me with their claws at the ready would be sitting. Among them was a girl who had lived across the street from my house; she played in one tone with one hand and another tone with the other, and at the end she wouldn't take her foot off the pedal but let the sounds float off like dust beaten out of the furniture.

In one of the boxes sat the artist who was so significant to me. I had met him when he was a schoolteacher. A few moments earlier he had stood onstage with a critic; after that he said some encouraging things to me, and it seemed that everything had to happen as if planned. But deep inside I privately retained the idea that it was going to be a disaster. Nevertheless I intended to plunge onstage as if into an illuminated swimming pool: I would try to hang on to that black piano as if I were fishing and had caught a shark. Who knew what might happen! Perhaps shark and audience would both be disconcerted by my audacity; my unexpected madness might strike them as original; once they got over being disconcerted, the public might begin to sympathize; my despair might succeed in improvising ways not strictly musical of arousing their interest.

When I was told that the house lights had been dimmed and I could get started, I went onstage with my head low, unloosing a few steps I had prepared as if I were setting a wind-up toy in motion. I didn't know what thought to attend to, but despite the agonizing velocity of things I had time to take note of my feet and move them in the direction of the piano.

Suddenly I found that the first rounds of applause and my first bows were over. I was sitting with my eyelids lowered, but my eyes were racing from side to side like dogs sniffing at everything; they ran across the keyboard and leapt into the piano, and I felt a confidence born from madness; at that point I was a little curious to see what the individual in the hand-me-down smoking jacket would do next. However unforeseen it all was, I knew that at the last minute he would raise his arms and hurl himself against the piano. I had experienced that once already, in the inland city where for the first time I had entertained an audience alone, with a piano in front of me.

For several months after that first concert, my job consisted of playing the piano in a dark dining room. Only one person listened to me. She had no interest in the fact that it was me who was playing. For my part, I played unwillingly. But during the pauses between the various pieces—when neither of us spoke—a silence would arise that set my thoughts working in unaccustomed ways.

One afternoon I'd gone to the Pianists' Association. The fellows there often found me work playing popular music with café orchestras, and they had sponsored my concert.

That afternoon, the head of the Association beckoned me aside, "*Che*, I have a little job for you. It isn't much" (he'd already begun adopting an expression that hinted at ulterior motives), "but there might be a great future in it for you. A rich widow wants someone to play for her twice a week. It's two one-hour sessions and she's paying one fifty per session."

At that point he broke off; they were calling him from the room next door and he went out for a moment.

He thought working for so little might depress me, and he said all this half-jokingly but in a tone that sought to be convincing; there wasn't much work around and I would be wise to take the first thing I found.

I would have been glad to confide how happy I was about this offer, but my need to go into unfamiliar houses would have been very difficult for me to explain and for him to understand. By the time he came back I was floating on a surge of vanity, thinking that the widow must have heard about my concert, or heard my name, or seen photographs or articles in the newspapers. Then I asked him, "She sent for me?"

"No, she sent for a pianist."

"To play good music?"

"I don't know. You'll have to work that out with her. Here's the address. Ask for Señora Muñeca."

The house had high marble balconies. As I stepped into the entryway I was stopped by its unaccustomed dimensions and its marble, which was finer than that of the balconies. The colors were indefinite; though they were right there they seemed to dwell in faraway places.

The beveled glass panes of the doors into the courtyard gazed at me; there was very little wood in them and they looked like ladies in low-cut dresses or with very long waists; the curtains were extremely delicate and made you feel you had startled the doors in their lingerie. Behind the curtains a fern, almost as tall as a palm tree and leaning slightly to one side, could be glimpsed.

A good while after I rang the bell I saw an enormous woman appear at the back of the courtyard. Until she opened the door I had a hard time convincing myself that she had a cigarette dangling from her lips. Without greeting me, she asked, "You're from the pianists' society?"

As soon as I answered she opened the door, turned around, and walked into the courtyard as if indicating that I should follow. The memory of her mouth as she spoke to me stayed on in my eyes: her lips were fleshy and the lit cigarette bobbed up and down between them. She led me to a corner of the courtyard that wasn't visible from the front hall. I sat down in a chair she designated with a lowering of her eyelids and asked her, "Are you Señora Muñeca?"

"If Señora Muñeca heard you say that, she'd throw us both out. But don't get nervous, I've taken care of everything."

She opened the door to the dining room. A landscape with storks was etched into its glass. The woman's head reached the level of a stork on the glass that had a fish in its beak and was about to swallow it.

I barely had time to look around the spacious courtyard, full of plants and colorful majolica; the blonde woman immediately reappeared with a small dessert plate. She sat down on the chair next to mine and put the plate on another chair. Then she said, "She won't be much longer. I've gotten her into the habit of ringing the doorbell when she comes home. I told her that if we left the door open she could be robbed."

I went to speak and couldn't find my voice, as though I were having to rummage for its sound in one of my pockets.

"She has good taste . . ."

She didn't let me finish.

"It isn't her taste. A 'dotor' used to live here. One of his daughters died, and he sold the house to Muñeca, who's been a widow and rich since she was very young."

She tapped the ash from her cigarette onto the dessert plate and I thought the plate was about to fall.

"What the 'dotor' didn't have was a piano. She bought the one in there, and quite a few tears it cost her."

I watched her, with my eyes and maybe even my mouth open. She seemed to like my way of listening, because after all her contemptuous silence she was very chatty until the mistress of the house arrived. What made her most talkative was anything to do with Señora Muñeca; even if she started out talking about something else, she would slowly slip back to the same subject, apparently without realizing it.

"Is Señora Muñeca as tall as you are?" I asked.

She laughed.

"When we moved here I had to lower all the mirrors; I'm the one who has to stoop."

Abruptly she started talking about the piano again: it was as if she'd left something on the stove and had to go back now and stir it.

"A lot of tears that piano cost her. She bought it for a former gentleman friend of hers to play. He composed a tango and named it 'Muñeca,' after her. Then one night when he was leaving for Buenos Aires, he didn't want her to see him off. She had a sudden urge to do it anyway, and the two of us went. He got to the boat late, and on the arm of another woman, and they ran up the gangplank together." I made a gesture as if to grab the plate—I thought it was falling. She understood and told me not to worry, but then the bell rang and she dashed out with the plate, reintroducing herself into the landscape of the storks.

A few moments later, I managed to make out a violet shape pressed against the front door. Impatient fingernails were tapping the glass. When the tall woman opened up, a short woman came in, speaking to her about the butcher. It seemed to me that one of the newcomer's eyes was looking over toward me. I saw her in profile; though she was of a certain age she didn't seem ugly, but I remember what happened when she started turning her face slowly toward me and I began to see her from the front. Her face was so thin that it gave me a disappointment of the kind that houses seen from the front give when, viewed from the side, they turn out not to have a rear but simply to end in a very sharp angle. It could almost be said that this face existed only in profile; seen from the front it was only a little bit wide at the eyes. Moreover, she was wall-eyed: the left eye looked forward and the right one looked off to the side. To compensate for the narrowness of her face, she piled her hair up into a great promontory in which various colors appeared: black, several shades of brown, and a few dirty locks that tended toward white. On top of all this sat a little bun, which offered a sampler of all the colors in close-knit synthesis.

When she began walking toward me, we looked at each other without speaking, and stayed that way all the time it took her to cross the courtyard.

"You're the pianist? Would you like to come in?"

She bore the promontory toward the door of the dining room. Despite all the hair, she barely reached the feet of the stork with the fish in its beak. When we pulled back the chairs from the big table, the sound echoed like a roar. That dining room, where little light came to illuminate the dark furniture, had a silence all its own. It pained me to hear the woman violate it when she said, "In my family" (her eyes were moving and I didn't know which of them to look at because I didn't know which one was looking at me) "in my family, all of us have had respect for music. And I want *music to be played* twice a week in this house."

She was called away just then because the butcher had come. As she stood up, she toyed with a long gilded chain that took various turns around her chest and finally came to an end attached to the left side of her belt.

Propped up on the sideboard were two oval trays that faced the courtyard and gathered from it the dining room's only remaining light. The fish in a painting that hung above the sideboard also gleamed faintly. The palm of my hand was numb because I'd been rubbing it against the tablecloth, which was now dark green. When she came back, I tried to hurry the interview along.

"What type of music does the señora wish to hear?"

"What do you mean what type of music? The kind of music everyone plays, the music that's in style."

"Very well. May I try out the piano?

"You should have done that already."

"Where is it?"

"Behind you. Don't you see it?"

"No, señora; there's not much light."

She pushed aside a screen that stood in the corner where the piano was. I tripped, and began muttering to myself. When I found the switch, light shone on the cherry-colored wood of a very small piano. After I had tried it out, and had emitted another "very well," it occurred to me to ask, "At what interval should I play the pieces?"

"What do you mean?"

"How many minutes should go by after I finish one piece and . . ."

"The same as at the Japanese Café."

I said a final "very well" and bade goodbye until the appointed day.

Señora Muñeca wasn't home the afternoon I arrived to play for the first time, either. The tall woman led me into the dining room and began serving up her chatter. She was named Filomena, but ever since she was a little girl she'd made everyone call her Dolly, which was the name of an unfortunate woman in a movie of that period who threw herself into the sea. As far as I could ascertain later, neither she nor the mistress of the house knew that Dolly is the English word for a little *muñeca*. And I was afraid—I don't know why—to rescue them from this ignorance. The last thing Dolly told me was about Señora Muñeca's brother. The señora had made him find a job, and if he went on behaving "properly" she would put a little house she had in the Prado, next to a chalet that also belonged to her, in his name.

The palm of my hand had gone numb again because I'd been rubbing it against the embossed surface of a nearby chair.

When Señora Muñeca rang the bell, I carried my chair over to the piano, put the sheet music on the stand and waited for her, ready to start. As soon as she came in, she raised her hands to her left side and unhooked the end of the chain, where she carried a little watch; it was as disproportionate as using a dungeon's chain to leash a tiny dog. "You may begin," she told me. Then she sat down at the other end of the table and had the idea, as I'd had, of running her hand over the tablecloth.

I started playing a tango, but before it was over the big woman appeared; she spoke loudly, to make herself heard over the sound of the piano. "Muñeca, where did you leave the kettle?"

Muñeca had a different sense of what was taking place; it had been her idea to have music played, and she was paying for it: a serious thing, as if she were having a play performed for herself. And then this other woman comes in and interrupts the performance, breaking off the sense of dignity and aristocracy that she wanted in her house. She stood up angrily and said, "Do not ever come in here and interrupt the music with your shouting."

The big woman turned and left. But almost at once Señora Muñeca called her back, shouting "Dolly!"

Right away the other woman answered, "Muñeca?"

"Prepare some *mate*. The kettle is in the bathroom."

I'd finished playing the tango; I was looking at the furniture and thinking about the doctor. There was something about that house that was like a sacred tomb abandoned in haste. And then these two women had settled into it, profaning the memories. On the sideboard was an open packet of *yerba mate*, and crystal goblets were stacked one on top of the other so that a bottle of ordinary wine could fit into the display cabinet.

Dolly silently brought in what she'd been asked for; I began playing a "valse sentimentale" and no one said another word. Señora Muñeca drank her *mate*, looked out towards the courtyard, and seemed, like the trays, to do nothing more than receive the day's last light. I did not ask for the floor lamp to be switched on. I played some pieces from memory and in the intervals I thought about things of my own. Señora Muñeca did not appear to hear the music; she had also stopped drinking the *mate* and one of her hands was resting motionless on the tablecloth.

At the following sessions, she had everything ready in advance. And after Señora Muñeca had drunk the first *mates* and I had played the first tangos she would remain immobile and I would think about my own affairs.

When I'd been working there for more than a month, it happened once more that Señora Muñeca's *mate* wasn't ready to be served. She came over to me a little nervously and told me she would hear me just as well from another room. That afternoon, she again told Dolly to make some *mate*, and that the kettle was in the bathroom. When Dolly came back and the señora was not in the dining room, she seized the chance to tell me: "It was two years ago today that we saw Muñeca's gentleman friend climbing the gangplank of the steamer with the other woman on his arm. So you take care, and be good."

She addressed me intimately as *tú*, which greatly displeased me, and I was preparing to reproach her for it when the señora arrived. That afternoon she appeared and disappeared like a light rain interrupted by sunshine.

A few days later, the Pianists's Association sent for me and the manager said, "Señora Muñeca was here, asking for a different pianist. She says you're a sad sack and your music isn't cheerful. I told her, 'Look, señora, he's the best pianist in the association,' and tried to make her change her mind by promising you would change your repertory and put more life into your playing."

I was depressed. It took a violent effort to force myself to show up for the next session, when I would have to "put more life" into my playing and, what was more, instruct Dolly not to address me as *tú*. But when I arrived in the dining room, unexpected things happened. Señora Muñeca's brother had come to visit and he turned out to be an acquaintance of mine. He stood up at once and held out his hand, "How are you, maestro? Congratulations— I know your concert was a great success. I saw the articles and photographs in the newspapers."

Muñeca's eyes were shooting off looks in all directions; crossing her eyes now seemed a deliberate way of evincing her distrust of everyone. Then she interrupted us, exclaiming, "What? They didn't tell me you were someone who appears in the newspapers!"

"Yes, of course!" her brother went on, "And we once appeared together in the same newspaper: we were separated only by a column. It was when I was appointed secretary of the club."

Muñeca intervened, "And the president congratulated you." Then she said, "You come along now"—addressing me as *tú*.

I had lowered my head, and saw first the violet dress and then, a short way behind, her brother's black pants leaving the dark dining room.

Then I began to remember the café where I was playing when I first met him. I don't know why they used to call him "Arañita" or "Spider Boy" or why he tolerated that when he was such a tough guy. And now I was stubbornly determined to make Señora Muñeca, with her violet dress, fit into this man's story. She was coming late to my idea of him, and though it would have been easier to leave the task for another day I couldn't keep from imagining once more all that I knew about Arañita, and adding this sister to it. But she was the one, it seemed to me, who was pushing her way into the story as forcefully as if it were a crowded bus.

The café was hidden behind some trees and beneath a row of second-floor balconies. Anyone who tried to go in was stopped by the door. When you put your hand on the handle, which was large and black like the handle of a tailor's iron, it turned in all directions without the least resistence. The door seemed to be laughing at you. If anyone inside happened to be standing a few steps from the window—and the glass was so dirty that if he were farther away you wouldn't see him—he might make a gesture with his arm as if to say, "Come on! Push!" Then you shoved and the door groaned but yielded. Once you were inside and had turned your back on the street, the door took its revenge by springing shut with a slam.

Most of the dim light given off by the few small lamps was swallowed up by the smoke, along with most of the colors of the clothing. The smoke also swallowed the small columns of the platform where we played. There were three of us: a "violin," a "flute" and me. It looked as though the smoke was what had raised our platform up near the white ceiling. Like employees of the sky, we sent our music down through the clouds and those below didn't seem to hear it. As soon as we finished a number we were invaded by the chatter of all those people. It was a strong, uniform murmur, and in winter we were overcome with drowsiness. Perched on the platform's railing, we would lean down, and I don't know what we would do for all that time with our eyes on the things below. Sometimes we simply watched how the heads down there bent foward into the white circles of the marble tables and how the hands lifted the coffees, which looked like small dabs of black, up towards the noses. One of the waiters was nearsighted and moved around behind a pair of thick glasses which would advise him, very slowly, of where he might find a thing, whereupon his nose would oscillate like a compass until finally it pointed towards his objective. In one hand he carried a tray and with the other he groped his way through the crowd. He'd been divorced and remarried and his house was full of small children. We contemplated him as if he were a steamer navigating among islands, running aground every so often and unloading the orders in all the wrong ports.

That was at night. But in the vermouth section things were very different, and not only because we knew it wasn't night but an hour of the afternoon, or because there were different people there, drinking different things. When the hour arrived, people from the political club located over the café would come in. They filled up two tables in the back, and almost all of them were friends or admirers of Arañita. Before they were able to converse with him, they would watch him a while from afar, waiting for him to finish making cocktails behind the bar. At that hour, and only then, a bright light was switched on, illuminating the whiteness of Arañita's jacket, shirt and teeth. In contrast were his tie, his eyebrows, his eyes and his emphatically black hair. The mediating color was provided by his face: it was olive-toned or a bit darker in certain places, especially above the eyebrows, for his brows would have been enormous if he hadn't shaved them, leaving just two strips like shoelaces.

No part of his face seemed to move during the ceremony, and no one knew the precise moment when he picked up or put down a bottle; the eye could not synchronize the instant when he conferred momentum upon an object with the instant the object obeyed. The bottles, glasses, ice and strainers each seemed to have a life of its own and to have been schooled to live in freedom; it didn't matter if they failed to obey instantaneously; they were responsible and everything would take place in its own time. The only time the eye could satisfy its vulgar thirst for synchronicity was when Arañita was vigorously applying himself to the cocktail shaker. At one of those moments I happened to stroll by one of the rear tables and heard someone saying, "You can see he's a man of character, eh?"

Arañita knew which cocktail was most in demand at a given hour. He would prepare a number of glasses at the same time. After shaking the cocktail shaker he would distribute the liquid into each glass with a single, steady movement of his hand, and his precision made you think of the secrets of nature: each drop went into its glass corral as if by an instinct of its species. Having relieved the cocktail shaker of the first load—drops of a dark race, say—he would then mix up another one of a white race, and pour out the new family of drops the same way. Then came the moment we were waiting for. He would take a long-handled spoon and with a few quick, swirling strokes intermingle the families of drops in each glass, and the unexpected would happen: each glass made a different sound, and a music of chance would ensue. The only unforeseeable part of each day was the reconciliation of these apparently identical glasses with the secret of their different sounds.

Suddenly we'd see Arañita putting on his tight black jacket and his hat, with a brim as hard and flat as steel. He came around the outside corner of the bar, and the owner himself—a friend and coreligionary—would serve him a *caña*. The politicians were already on their way out and would be waiting for him at the club. During that hour, I would occasionally remember something I knew about him. He once had a lady friend who asked his permission to go to a dance; he said no but she went all the same. He soon found out and cut off relations with words that were like a quick sequence of sharp blows. She came to the café one afternoon, but he sent a waiter to show her out. Not long after that she took poison.

At first he was very friendly to us, but one fine day he stopped saying hello. Along the railing of our platform were rows of colored lights, and he was in charge of switching them on when the orchestra began to play. One day the "violin" discovered that Arañita would switch them on at the precise moment when the first chord of our first number rang out. Thinking we'd play a joke on him, we all played a single, random chord at the same time. The explosive chord combined with the light caught the crowd's attention and a few people applauded. But Arañita paced angrily up and down behind the bar and seemed ready to leap over it. He didn't say hello to us again after that, but a long time later when I was no longer playing at the café, he saw me in the street and came over to greet me with a big, open grin, and we became friends again.

He came to greet me in the dark dining room before he left that afternoon, as well, and told me, "You can relax. Your job in this house is secure."

Well, all right. That was one of the consquences of the concert. Then I realized that something else had been on my mind, but I couldn't remember what it was. I soon came up with it: Dolly should not address me as *tú*. And just at that moment she walked in, holding out her hand to me. She'd come running on tiptoe. There was nothing for me to do but give her my hand. Then she said, "Congratulations. *Te felicito*," and dashed back out.

In the subsequent sessions, Muñeca once again sat silently sipping *mate* in the dining room and I could think all I wanted about my own affairs.

After Arañita had arranged matters for me in his sister's house, Muñeca went for a long time without interrupting my thoughts. She would sip *mate* until the water had gone cold and then, letting her wandering eyes be still, she, too, gazed in upon her memories. But late one afternoon when the dining room was very dark and the session was almost over, Muñeca spoke to me. She was very far from my thoughts at that moment, and when her words crashed into me, collapsing the silence, I made a sudden movement with my feet and kicked the piano: the sounding board resonated and Muñeca let out a tactless chuckle. Then she repeated her words, "I was asking what the little tango you just played is called."

My first impulse was to tell her the title, but then I thought that if I said it—the tango was called "You're Gone? Ha-ha . . ."— she'd think it was an allusion to the man who walked up the gangplank with another woman. So I turned on the light and was about to carry the sheet music over to her, but she saw what I intended to do and stopped me, "No, no. Just tell me what it is."

I uttered it in a strange voice; she made me repeat it and then said, "*Jesús*! It's a title for Carnival."

I didn't want that title to bring back bad memories. Yet I was attracted by dramas that happened in other people's houses; one of the hopes my concert had aroused was that I would make new acquaintances who would give me access to unfamiliar houses.

One afternoon when I was thinking about the drama of other people's lives I smelled a strong odor of roast pork in the dark dining room. I said to Dolly, "What a smell of roast pork! Why don't you take that out of here? It's a pity . . . Such a lovely dining room . . . !"

She was angry. "And what's wrong with having the dining room smell of pork? Would you"—*tú*, she said—"rather I put it in the parlor?"

There it was on the sideboard on a blue enamelled platter, protected by a piece of white cheesecloth. Dolly left, but then came back a while later and said, "I know you want to eat some of that pork." (*Tú* again.)

I began protesting strongly but she talked back, she wanted to shut out my voice and was trying to grab hold of my hands. As I was moving them out of her reach and she was pursuing them, our blind grabs made patterns in the air and I felt the breeze from our four hands on my flushed face. Finally I put my hands behind my back and resigned myself to what Dolly was saying.

"*Mirá:* come over by the back way at ten o'clock, there's a tree back there with thick branches that reach up near the little window in the kitchen. I won't let you in by the front door because people might gossip, and I have a gentleman friend and am thinking of getting married."

I wanted to interrupt her but she managed to seize one of my hands. I snatched it away and while I was still thinking about how rude my gesture had been, she went back to her explanation, "You climb the tree, and come in the window at ten; I'll have the pork ready along with a liter of wine—you'll see what a party we'll have."

Finally she gave me a chance to say, "And what if Muñeca hears me? Do you think I'm going to lose this job over a slice of roast pork?"

She gazed at me for a few moments in puzzled silence. Then she said, "By nine-thirty, I've put Muñeca to bed and she's fast asleep; I could wait until morning to take her clothes off."

"She sleeps as soundly as that?"

Dolly started chortling, then sat down, took a pair of red shoes off her feet, shoved them under the legs of her chair, and told me, "As soon as you leave she starts drinking wine, then she drinks wine with dinner, after dessert she goes on drinking wine, and when she's good and drunk I take her up to bed."

Dolly gazed at my face, was encouraged, and went on talking. "Forever telling me to do things the proper way, all those aristocratic airs, not letting me have a moment's conversation with anyone who visits her, not even her brother, and then she gets drunk as a sow."

I lowered my head and she asked, "So what'll it be? Are you coming to have some pork with me or not?"

I begin improvising clumsy excuses; the worst one was that I might fall out of the tree. She understood, pursed her lips to one side, put her shoes back on, and said as she was leaving, "*Andá, andá*, they picked you when you were still green."

One afternoon not much later, Dolly did not come out to greet me. A manservant with sideburns, a vest and striped sleeves appeared. He handed me a letter in which Muñeca informed me that my services had been suspended and enclosed the money she owed me.

After that I went without work for a while. I was almost ready to climb the tree in the hope of seeing Dolly.

One summer morning I was full of pessimism and thought about all my failures. Not only had that first concert not brought me any money, it hadn't brought me any of the things I'd been hoping for. Not even new acquaintances so that I could go into unfamiliar houses; the house with the dark dining room had been the only one, and there I'd had only a faint suspicion of drama when I learned that Muñeca got drunk, while Dolly didn't seem to be a woman of any drama at all.

I was dragging these thoughts slowly behind me as I strolled along a stretch of the Prado with my hands behind my back when I felt someone tickling the palm of my hand. I turned and found Dolly. She said, "I saw you go past the house and followed you."

"What? You're not working for Muñeca anymore?"

"That old woman will remember me all her life. One afternoon, I told her, 'Start looking for someone else. I'm leaving tomorrow.' She answered, 'Now what did I do to you?' So I sprang this on her: 'Nothing this time, but I'm getting married . . . to your brother.' A strange trembling came over her and she started foaming at the mouth because that very morning she'd made that little house over to her brother."

We'd gone on walking. But when she reached the part about Arañita I stopped to look at her. She took my hand and said,

"Come and have a look at the house. Arañita is always at work at this hour."

I withdrew my hand and said, "No. Some other day."

The anger she'd felt when I hadn't wanted to climb the tree returned; curling her upper lip, she told me, "*Andá, andá,* go on with you, go on, you poor pianist."

In that dark dining room, I acquired a new way of thinking about my contradictions. It seemed strange that in my own house, and amid so much distress, we'd had moments of happiness. I'm referring to the days before my concert in Montevideo, before we sold the furniture and the family broke up. We'd made one of our last efforts to reunite, but my wife and daughter were still far from Montevideo. I'd come to the capital city after working at seaside resorts and inland cities. At the same time, I'd been preparing for the concert and holding out many hopes for the various consequences it might have.

During that period, each of us in the house tried to conceal his individual distress, but there were also general distresses.

The back of our house had a charm that could momentarily stave off all thoughts of unhappiness. It gave onto a small forest of immense trees. We clutched the wire fence with our hands and sent our eyes off into the distance, all the way to where the tree trunks mingled with the paths. Far above our heads were many tender young leaves that had no notion of the wire fence and leaned towards our house. We drank in their shade in silence. But suddenly the front doorbell would ring and the shade would be embittered. It was the men who were after my father for debts. My father was a good man, but his accounts came out badly. He worked very hard and ran around everywhere in constant comings and goings to keep himself from sudden collapse: he was finishing up as the owner of a construction company.

The doorbell rang at every hour of the day; only at night—very late at night—did its sound die out.

The company's death throes were long and the shouts of those who came to collect what they were owed grew louder all the time. One day he was sick but wanted one of those men to come in. As the shouting grew louder the family walked toward the bedroom, then surrounded the bed, and finally the man left, taking his curses and threats with him out into the street. That lasted a few months; exactly the same months it took me to make the final preparations for my concert.

The night of the concert, before falling asleep—at that point I was staying at a friend's house—I began seeing Señora Muñeca's dining room. I thought about the life of those pieces of furniture and remembered the furniture in my own house. Who knew where it was now: we'd had to send it to an auctioneer the day before my concert; the time period my father had been granted to vacate the house—he couldn't pay the rent—had expired, and we'd had to sell the furniture.

I remembered our happiness as if I were peering through a small hole: I could see the back of my house under a bright light, and I remembered a moment, around noon, when I'd just come back from a city in the interior and my family hadn't seen me yet. They were sitting around the table, which they had set outside under the trees, and I, without being there with them yet, knew that the tablecloth was dappled with large coins of light and shadow, mingling and merging at the least movement of air among the leaves. They were busy with their little meal and their little bit of happiness and seemed to have forgotten me. Still, before they saw me, I succeeded in forming an absurd idea: I thought that the moment was like a memory I would have many years later, when I had outlived them all.

On some afternoons in the dark dining room that instant was

what I most remembered: at every moment my family was having lunch again in that landscape and I was thinking again that they had forgotten me.

That same night, after a short dream, I woke up and opened my eyes in the darkness; I remembered that I was in an unfamiliar bed; I thought of the dispersed fragments of my family; and suddenly I went back to what had happened one afternoon in the dark dining room. I hadn't understood Muñeca. If my friend had known her— the one who'd been my teacher at school—perhaps he would have suspected something interesting about that life. Over the years of my friendship with him, my curiosity about other people's dramas had grown. And one of the most secret consequences I was hoping for from my concert was that he would introduce me to people I didn't know and I would go into unfamiliar houses. That was my most dangerous thought as I was preparing for my concert, and I didn't always manage to keep it at bay. I wished there were no drama in my own house, not only because of the suffering it caused us but also because I wanted to immerse myself in the dramas of others. I don't know why that gave me such great pleasure. Already, during the concert's intermission, I had been thinking about this, as if in the grip of an uncontrollable vice. When the concert began, I played the first notes; my fingertips punctured the silence. Though the concert hall was seeded with expectant ears, the severest critic was the silence; it opened a dark mouth that yawned far too wide as soon as the humblest sound appeared, making it run to join the other sounds. But later, once a certain sympathy had developed within the audience, the sounds waited for the silence to hush them with its cape.

At the end of each piece I did not stand up to bow, but inclined my torso forward while remaining seated. I'd seen a concert pianist do this a short while before and liked it. But during the intermission my friend, the teacher, came and told me, "*Che,* you have to stand up and spend more time with the public. Look at the girls."

That was when I couldn't hold back the thought of everything that must be hiding out there in the audience.

Soon after the concert was over I left the theater with my two painter friends. Over a long dinner they told me about the events of the evening and I listened to them with an attention that was not a pianist's kind of attention. Then we went home and lay down on mattresses on the floor. The painters and my brother played at imitating animals until suddenly all three bodies formed a single mass in their struggle, but I couldn't take part because I was exhausted. I barely smiled. They went to sleep; I didn't. I was beginning to wait for the consequences of my concert.

I slept very little, and the following morning, when the sun was already streaming in through the blinds, I saw a mouse that had approached the sleeping head of one of the painters and was eating his hair.

Note:

"My First Concert in Montevideo" was not published during Felisberto's lifetime. According to Paulina Medeiros, the story was originally much longer, but on the advice of Jules Supervielle, Felisberto carved two other stories—"My First Concert" and "The Dark Dining Room," which later appeared in the collection *No One Lit the Lamps*—out of it, and left the rest, probably intending to polish it further at some point.

José Pedro Díaz, editor of the first edition of Felisberto's complete works (Montevideo: Arca, 1967–74), was the first to piece the story together from six typed pages and some cut and pasted fragments of other pages that were found among Felisberto's papers. The order of the original manuscript pages is open to debate, however, and several different arrangements have been proposed. The version that appears here follows the one in the Siglo Veintiuno edition of Felisberto's complete works (Mexico City, 1983), edited by María Luisa Puga.

MISTAKEN HANDS

IRENE:

Don't worry. Which is to say that I'd like you to worry a little, if there were some curiosity in your worry. Curiosity is precisely the reason I wanted to write you—I'll soon explain this attitude in all possible detail—but first I must promise that I won't embarrass you; anyone can read what I write and they'll find nothing but curiosity in it—and what's more, since your name was chosen at random from among many, a free curiosity. I had no prior inclination towards your person, but your name, chosen from so many, was the first thing in the unknown that my curiosity paused over. I also encountered the unknown in the movement my curiosity made when it alit on your name. And I always encounter the unknown in the depths of my own curiosity. You'll find the little I know about my own curiosity in the story I've promised; I insist on telling it to you because it's important that my approach cause you as little awkwardness as possible. However, the hope that the person I'm addressing this letter to might undergo a similar curiosity was what first prompted me to begin writing it.

For many years, until a few months ago, my madness wandered among the sciences. There, too, I felt curiosity and there, too, I sensed the unknown. But one night, as I was distractedly gazing out from my house into the street—it was almost dark and a few people were going by—my curiosity and interest in the unknown began to change: they turned towards the people passing by. A few of those people were hunched over, and I felt the desire to know what they were feeling and thinking at that moment. However absurd it was to aspire to know what that might be, from that night on the desire was in me. The following morning, shortly after I woke up, a headlong urge to leave my house came over me—to see what the people riding in the same buses as me and crossing paths with me on the streets were like. Starting that day, I was interested in seeing and feeling the movement of the streets, with their people and things, from early in the morning. I walked among the people as carelessly as if I were still at home getting ready to go out. I wasn't looking for anything, and I knew I would find something; I was already finding it: the unknown. I'd given myself over to it that night in my house with my arms propped on the wooden railing, when I first began to see the passers-by as strange figures, far more distant and unknown than ever before. The next morning they were just as strange, unknown, and distant to my eyes, despite the daylight and the fact that I'd joined them in their passage along the streets, and they stood so close to me in the buses.

But by the evening of that same day I realized that the unknown appears more often at night than during the day: at night I felt a darkness around my spirit, as well. However clear my thoughts were, something of what the night and my spirit suggested was reaching them. The darker the air, the greater the suggestion of the unknown. And if that air reached places where there were lamps, it didn't matter. Even if I was distracted or thinking of something else, I could feel that beyond the lamps' light was that same air still charged with darkness. I also came to understand that the unknown was furtive: it passed by in the depths of a street; next to a train crossing through; when I thought I had run into someone I knew who turned out not to be that person; at a moment when a woman in a movie theatre turned her head back and looked around as if searching for someone; as several people emerged from a doorway; when the figures of two little girls, like small, newly lit flames, appeared on a corner I'd glanced at a moment earlier; when a woman let out a laugh and then stifled it with her handkerchief; when two strangers were speaking nearby about someone I knew; when, going home late at night, I suddenly thought I saw the face of a man who'd been dead for some time; and in so many other strangely incoherent things.

Another night I realized something else about the unknown: it doesn't always collide with me out of nowhere; sometimes it arrives as if I were sleeping and begins by putting very light blankets on me and then heavier and heavier ones until I wake up and throw them all off.

Once I was sitting in a theater, in the middle of the first ring, and I saw in the orchestra section the back of a black velvet jacket from which a blond head and a pair of arms and hands gloved in white kid emerged. Distractedly I watched the movements of that head and those arms, and little by little I came to feel that someone else had seen those movements, that strange grace, in one of his dreams . . . Then the curtain rose and I turned my attention to the stage.

Another time, in a very luxurious and almost vacant movie theater, I gradually began to feel an inexplicable anguish: the sumptuousness itself was creating that anguish in me, and in that sumptuousness was a strange silence . . . But another evening I found myself feeling that same unknown anguish in a drawing room full of happy voices and beautifully dressed women—and what was more, in that same lively drawing room, the unknown also fleetingly appeared: in the moment when a woman made a movement that would have struck even her as strange, if she had seen it; in the way someone looked at other people who had just come in; in an unknown signal from a woman's slender hand. . . .

I interrupted this letter when a friend came to fetch me to go to a party. Someone there, commenting on the colors a woman had painted around her eyes, uttered her name. My heart stopped. And as I was verifying that there couldn't be two people with this name, I began thinking once more about the unknown. For wasn't meeting her while I was composing a letter to her as a complete stranger yet another aspect of the unknown? Then, after we were introduced and had talked for a long time, I realized how many marvelously unknown things are in you, and I thought that what remained to be said in my letter was becoming easier: for I want to ask you to surrender a few of the moments when you feel this thing I'm saying over and over until it grows tiresome—this vulgar word, "unknown." Would it interest you to write the history of those moments?

The postman arrives at the house at twilight. At that hour I'll be thinking you might write me.

Best wishes.

Inés:

I woke up late today. But I didn't get out of bed right away because I had to remember what happened last night. And since the person wearing mourning clothes last night was you—and the other people and the noise and the light all had the jumbled quality of an old movie—I felt that if I got up to write you a letter I would have the privilege of addressing myself to a vague figure out of a dream. But before I got up, my attention fell on the red carnation on my lapel, and it seemed to me that my suit belonged to the personage who spoke to you last night, to that "I" who was also made from a dream.

Things welled up out of you that I remember less for your words than for the way you held yourself as you talked, and when I was talking I felt as if I wasn't speaking at all but only continuing to feel what you'd been saying with your gestures.

Through the loose weave of your hat brim, the light cast arabesques of shadow on the upper part of your face, and the brightness of your very white teeth seemed to have nothing to do with your black eyes, gleaming through the shadowy arabesques. But when we left the bar and were walking together the shadows moved, and as we passed beneath the streetlights, a mask seemed to fall from the top of your face.

I also feel the shadow of a dream when I remember how the two of us walked: no sooner were we side by side than our companions separated us and we were at opposite ends of the group. But suddenly, quickening my pace a bit, I saw you addressing me with your gestures, and soon found myself at your side. Later, I'd gone far ahead with a companion; we were called back because some people were about to leave the group, and then, finding myself beside you again and seeing you without the hat, and with that hair, I felt something that was like the epilogue of that night.

A few days have gone by. I haven't wanted to stir up my memories, preferring to let them sleep, but they have dreamed.

It's now twenty-four hours since I saw you in the street, wearing a different hat. I'm very far away, it's nighttime, and the present seems like a dream. How can it be that I met you once again, that you were wearing a different hat, and that I had to leave Montevideo that very night? The friend I had to go with was departing from the city only a few hours after you took your leave of me without knowing it. I remembered all this in a lonely and picturesque place I've never been before, and that's what makes the present a dream.

This afternoon, passing through a marvelous place where a stream runs through the forest, I thought that if possible I would return to that spot to read a letter you would send me, and until it comes I'll be busy waiting for it. Will you write me soon?

The wishes I gave you last night still surround me, and I still have yours.

To Inés:

For many days now I've been doing things that I somehow feel to be external to me; even when they're spontaneous and linked to my innermost being, I experience them as if they were outside me: this happens when I'm with my friends, and when I play the piano. But in the very scarce moments when I find myself alone, before I fall asleep and just before I get up, I feel that—even when I'm not thinking about it—what began that night has been taking shape within me.

That second night when you were wearing a different hat was the first time I became aware of it. It had been growing, hidden in the many moments when I wasn't thinking about it, and when I met you it surprised me in a very strange way: I felt that without my knowledge a space had been prepared within me where the emotion of that meeting would fall and stay, as if locked up.

Since then, in the space where that emotion fell, a feeling has been taking shape, a feeling always close to me even when I don't remember it exists. It suddenly appears and surprises me with a gentle throb. Then I leave a silence in the middle of a conversation, or I grow distracted, or I experience the piece I'm playing on the piano with greater intensity.

At times, when this gentle throb comes, I think I've been waiting for it unknowingly, but at other times it takes me as unaware as if I were to roll over and see a great, formless shadow opposite my bed; then the shadow changes, but I never succeed in foreseeing the direction from which the light is hitting me, or where my shadow will fall. . . .

The day your letter arrived—the letter that is now mine and for which I have such high regard and respect—the throbbing was no longer gentle.

Intense wishes.

Irene:

Desire has given me a habit of writing you some of the things I feel and think. But neither what I myself think, nor what intelli-

gent men think, nor what the wise discover—though all that interests me a great deal—is what I prefer to encounter in my life.
Which is not to say that I wouldn't sometimes like to step inside
the moments when intelligent men's thoughts take strange turns
and get lost . . . the moments of wise men's impassioned stub-
bornness as they seek.

I'll have to fall back on thought, however, in order to tell you
what I like best to encounter: still those same things that belong to
the unknown. My madness makes me seek them everywhere, and
I'm still seeking them, in cheap novels, even if they're tawdry and
false, and in great works, although their authors are very deft at
handling thought—but there are always moments when the author
didn't seem to know that some unknown thing remained, moments
left there in passing, when he wrote something he wasn't proud of
and may never refer to or recite from memory.

That night I reached the movie theater after the picture had
started, and as long as I hadn't yet grasped the plot I felt the unknown. Sometimes I feel it in spite of the plot, too, and those slight
possibilities are the reason I always go to the movies.

Once I wrote two fragments with very little in them produced
by thought and very little purpose——but they contain what I like
to find.

Things I would like to happen
I would be sitting on the grass in the woods.

I would be thinking of other things that had nothing to do with
the woods.

But suddenly I would be distracted and would scan the great
trees from top to bottom.

After that, the trees' great trunks would interrupt my view of
the people going by some distance away.

One of those people would stir up some dust as he walked, and
I would realize that he was walking down a dusty path.

But before I'd finished imagining that path, a young woman would go by.

She would be pretty, but I wouldn't know where she was going or why she was almost running.

It wouldn't occur to me to follow her, but not because I was finding my idleness so pleasant: perhaps I would see the woman again some other day.

I would get up from the grass and then I would be somewhere else.

But that woman and the other things about those woods would slumber in my forgetting mind until who knows when.

It would be night.

I would be arriving from the darkness of a highway lined with farms.

When I reached an intersection with a well-lit, cobbled street, I would feel as though I were stepping onto a stage with many eyes fixed upon me: then I would stop at one of the corners as if waiting for something.

No one would look at me, though there was a thronging tavern across the way.

A man near the tavern, in the posture of someone waiting for a streetcar, would look at me; that man would be a playwright I've always wanted to meet, but the opportunity to be introduced to him had never arisen.

I'd look up. A light bulb would be strung up in the center of the crossroad.

The light, more powerful than the bulb, would be shining on the crowns of the paradise trees which were at that height.

Then the playwright would take the streetcar and I'd go into the tavern.

Now I feel like telling the story of the audacity that's led me to note down such simpleminded things here.

A long time ago I reflected that if our much-esteemed thought ever dreamed of setting forth concretely the order and just weight of all that is in the spirit, then perhaps, before its master died, the spontaneous forces of Nature would awaken him from his nightmare, and he would find that reality is sometimes intrinsically dark and confused. When writers and psychologists believe they've illuminated reality, they are referring to something else: they transform the dark reality into a bright reality and then it's no longer reality with its real color, quality, and condition—instead they set forth a reality of their own heads that has nothing to do with the events spontaneously occurring in the spirit.

In this real confusion, no sooner does vanity seem to take thought for its servant than thought seems to be the author of vanity, or that which makes vanity grow, etc. But in the end, I know that our much-esteemed thought does intervene in our sorrows, pleasures, and feelings, and does take risks so that our spirit will be superior and our personality prized. To some degree I would feel sympathy for this; it's only that when vanity predominates, and in turn makes thought predominate, then life is a singular torture. Often the torture cannot be withstood and in that case the patient is saved, but in other cases he endures the condition until death.

I had written this in a story:

"The man I was before I met her had the indifference of weariness. If I'd met her much earlier I would long since have expended my energies on loving her, but I didn't, so I expended those energies thinking: I thought so much that I discovered the vanity and falsity of thought, which takes itself for the primary guide of our destiny. Nevertheless I kept on thinking; my energies went on attacking my thoughts, and I felt the most uncongenial sort of weariness. The man I am now reposes in the anxiety of loving to his heart's content, but from the 19th of May, two days after the story began, until the 6th of June, the day I myself suspended the story because early the next morning I was leaving the city where she lived—in the twenty-two days between those two dates—I also reposed in her large blue eyes. The distance between her eyes and her brows, a space painted a delicate blue, was also large, and from that blue vault seemed to descend the thing in her eyes that made me rest from my thoughts and love her as fully as I liked."

Even after it has been exposed, thought persists and gives explanations for why it persists. I would have preferred not to write you about thought in this letter—but look how much I'm thinking in order to eliminate thought! This is the punishment of those who would attack it: to go on thinking. Nevertheless, my thought now gives me explanations—and goes on thinking—in order to write what it thinks in a medium that holds out a great many possibilities for eliminating thought. Furthermore, I have some hope that by strongly attacking thought right from the start, our letters will be freer of it. Indeed, the two little fragments I copied were quite free of it. But I haven't yet presented my defense for having copied them, though everything I've said so far is relevant to it.

While it's true that certain things remain in memory because of the intensity with which thought brings our feelings into play, it's also certain that other things in which thought has hardly any role remain there as well. This happens with childhood memories, and that—for I believe something in me has remained a child—is why I search with a particular simplicity; that is why I found that vein of the unknown which interests me. I also enjoy and am cheered by my memories of moments that had little or no significance, when I experienced life in a state quite free of thought or spiritual tension.

Furthermore, I don't believe that when thought seizes us it releases us so quickly. And I still want to add an epilogue, explaining more fully the object of everything thought has said—for the fact of having an object is a quality of thought. And I want to free our letters in every way possible of anything pertaining to thought. With respect to myself and this hope, I want to leave thought behind and keep it from attacking me as frequently in the future; with respect to the unknown, I want to define the vein more clearly by specifying that there is little thought in it; with respect to the memory of events, I want to depict those in which thought has had little part; with respect to what I noted down, I want to defend— for thought is a thing of attack and defense—the simplemindedness of the things I noted, and to defend myself as well from the lack of a connecting thread—for it is thought that threads things together. Finally, I want to know if this vein in which I propose that you write interests you, because I would never ask you to write on a preordained subject, even if I had some hope that you were suffering from the same curiosity as I am.

If you do write me, don't go to any effort; I would like it to become a carefree pleasure for you, and to have some of the wealth of feminine things that are in you when you play and your spirit is stirred by unexpected delights.

A great wish.

Margarita:

There's no need to read this story right away: I'd prefer you to read it at moments when you don't need to think about anything or feel like thinking about anything—although those are the moments when one thinks of these things. . . .

Not long ago, on the platform of a small station where I was waiting for a late train, some memories and thoughts joined together to make me understand how great one simple desire was in my life. The external result of this desire is that I take immense joy in writing and receiving certain letters. The feeling that gave rise to this desire is even simpler: a feeling of calm, slow delight that wants to go forth and encounter unexpected things and, at the same time, awaits them. The next day, when I was in my little house, in a calm and picturesque outlying neighborhood, there persisted still—as a child would persist in demanding to be told a story—that same immense desire to write and receive certain letters. And at once I began supposing to myself the emotion I would feel as I set down in a letter things I had felt in the solitude of my little house, as I went to send off my letter amid the clamor of the city, as I walked home imagining how my letter would reach the intimate solitude of a woman living among a multitude of strangers, and, finally, as I thought about the day when, in the tranquility of my picturesque neighborhood, the other letter would arrive, the one that would bear hidden within it some of the things that are to be hoped for.

All these conjectures were rather unclear. At times it seemed to me that they were awaiting the memory and conjecture of extraordinary women, and at other times that such memories and conjectures were vaguely and stealthily participating in them. But as my thoughts attacked the memories, the women I was imagining tended to disappear and those I knew to appear; then everything became clearer and more genuine; each of the women stood still, surrounded by the memories that corresponded to her. At times the memories of one got tangled up in those of another, and I pictured the two of them together in an interview; but I soon remembered conversations in which each one defended her charms, and saw them separately once more.

As I imagined how a letter from me would fall into each woman's mystery, I realized that however simple that mystery might be, it wouldn't be my fate to know the things produced in her spirit. And then an immense desire to experience that simple mystery, an immense desire to stir it up and see whether it was a friend of my own mystery, made me fall into the same place towards which my mingled thoughts and memories had been pushing me the day before, when I stood on the platform of a small station waiting for a train that would be late.

In the moments when I was thinking about the mystery of a woman, my premonitions were troubled. There was a doubleness in my mind: of knowing that a thing was, and wanting to know what form it had, of feeling that it existed, and wanting to feel its way of stirring and existing.

And I felt something else happening in my spirit, too, for I perceived neither limit nor distance at the moment when the premonition of another spirit's mystery occurred, and I felt the desire to reach that spirit by whatever means were required. Premonition and desire were more than linked, they were joined and intermingled at birth. I didn't know whether the premonition of a mystery awoke the desire to move toward it, or whether it was the desire that gave rise to my premonition of the mystery. But I knew for certain that all of this was the adventure my spirit most wanted, an adventure that began when those memories and thoughts joined together.

When I reached that point, I wanted to distract myself and stop thinking about this; I pretended to myself that I wanted to plan out the adventure, but I also felt something like a slight fear of wasting this emotion, for I might run out of it. Then, after mastering my desire to go on thinking about it, and while I was doing and thinking about other things, I was attacked by a curiosity—which was very prudent, though it contained some pent-up emotion—about who my first letter would be addressed to, and what things I would put in it.

That same night I felt very contented. I'd gone to the center of the city and found myself surrounded by clamor and people I knew. But then that night, that clamor, those people, and the bits of things I was hearing, produced a singular, ugly anguish in me—for I've experienced other moments of anguish which, in memory and even while I was feeling them, have had something good about them; they've belonged more fully to me, and I've even thought that my feelings somehow understood them, and the sadness they left in my memory had a refined quality—but the anguish I felt that night was a thing that did not belong to my life, a thing incomprehensible to my feelings, like a sickness for which my system had no predisposition, like something sent to me by mistake.

As I was going home on the streetcar, trying to shake off this singular, ugly anguish and distractedly watching the squares of light which the streetcar projected down the streets and up the sidewalks, a futile, false, and vicious thought came to me. I thought about what might happen if I revealed my secret to the people I knew, and the thought had all the vertigo and suggestive pull I would feel if I were to set my foot on the edge of a skyscraper's roof, yet it was useful because it led me to other thoughts that made me see many of the obstacles to be overcome before my letters could fall into the abyss of the mystery of extraordinary women. I also thought about many difficulties that were unrelated to such women, but brought me some knowledge of the common reactions of the spirit. However much culture and intelligent freedom there may be in a person, the tiniest unaccustomed event occurring in another's spirit in relation to her own will produce at least a slight reaction, and that reaction may be enough to inhibit her spontaneity. It is less than habitual for a man to write to a woman without the occasion of even the most insignificant concrete event and for no reason but an inspired desire to see how another person experiences life, stirring up her mystery to see if it is a friend, and to feel all the things I've tried to express. It is also uncommon for someone to feel, as I do, a desire so simple.

Something similar happens when two people meet and one becomes attached to the other, but that's more frequent and wouldn't strike anyone as strange. Still, that spontaneous movement of the spirit is very similar to what I feel now as I write—any difference there may be is not one of attitude. My desire could be continuous with that other desire, for after two people speak and feel some

premonition of affinity, it's very natural for them to enjoy exchanging sensations of thought and spirit at a distance. The exchange would depend on the velocity of the people in question; it's
possible that for those of us who are slow, and whose sensations
proceed slowly, every event in the spirit lasts longer and is accompanied by more commentary than in people of rapid sensations;
thus, for us slow ones, distance gives communication a whole new
array of nuances, and could even offer some compensation for
whatever might happen in the flesh at close proximity. And, too,
though we draw many things from the depths of our experience
when we're improvising in the presence of another person, it's also
possible that our improvisation may lead us to betray even the best
of what we know to be true, and certain details might interfere
with the feeling of truth. Not that I don't believe in the good
things that are part of a live exchange—all the mystery that physical presence can begin to elicit, or even the good effect its distur-
bances have on the spirit, stirring it up and giving rise to other
possibilities—but there are souls in which the memory of presence
produces a different sort of nuance and enriches feelings with new
elements and all the unknown that distance conjures up, as we
somehow reconstruct the physical presence we do not have.

On several occasions I've been very happy speaking with you
about the events that take place in the spirit, and that's why I now
intensely desire the great, restful pleasure of doing so in this other
way. I've told you this story to make you fully aware of my desires
and give you as little reason as possible to react against them.

Though the letters I really want to write are free of expecta-
tions, this one is intended to ask you to please write me letters, and
therefore I would like this one to be the prologue. I ask for nothing
but what I've given you first here: commentaries on things. Although the last time I saw you, you reacted by telling me you
weren't in the habit of answering letters, I still hold out the hope
that you'll write me: this letter does not possess the merit of hav-

ing been written in the certainty of going unanswered—there, do you see how frankly I'm speaking to you? For it would give me immense delight if this letter were deserving enough to persuade you to make an exception to your rule: and though I know how strong the inertia of your life is within you, I cannot easily renounce so immense a desire.

Irene:

I don't quite recall if you'd already closed your little umbrella while my big one was still open, when we spoke about the man I admired and loved so much in my childhood. But I well remember that standing next to you there beneath the intermittent rain and the streetlight and the green of the trees, I felt the unknown I tried so hard to speak of in my letters. I felt the pressure of the unknown most strongly while recollecting that man, who no longer exists; and the dusk, with its indefinite rain and artificial light and trees and all the rest, formed a scene that would make me go back to those memories later. As I experience that twilight now, it seems much closer to the period when he lived than to the present in which we happened to encounter each other a few days ago. But for a moment this era when I'm still living and he is not seemed to have something false about it: there would be a price to pay, something serious that would happen to me, for the privilege of existing when he no longer did. Yet I felt the present, too: when I was falling into your eyes with my eyes, I remembered how black and deep his eyes were, and that was when I felt the unknown with the greatest intensity: the unknown was looking out at me through those eyes. But at the same time there was something else in your eyes and face, something that made me overcome my momentary feeling of how false the present was, and forced the unknown to begin anew. While we were speaking, there was something that had nothing to do with words; the words served to attract us to each other's silence. Now I feel as though I'm maintaining that silence, and writing in it. But during that twilight, even as I was speaking and anxiously developing my thoughts, I could feel the presence of other thoughts, and I felt those thoughts appearing and disappearing, as if I were riding a horse very fast along a forest path, thinking of nothing but arriving, and other horsemen suddenly passed nearby and were lost among the trees and then appeared once more.

At times, among all the words in my conversation, one would make you smile; then I would look in wonder at your face, as if it were a lake into which I'd accidentally dropped some object, and I could see the ripples it produced without knowing what the object had been.

Now I'm greatly inclined to remember certain things and little inclined to write. And you, in your silence, are you writing or not?

Margarita:

It must have been around four o'clock this afternoon when the glad young words sent by your hands came to visit me. I recognized them from afar because, as always, they came inside a little blue envelope. It's now eleven o'clock, and their visit has not yet ended.

Just before nightfall, a messenger knocked on my front gate: he was bringing me a letter from a lady friend. I thought your letter's words might take advantage of that moment to leave, but immediately I felt them laughing in my head. Will they spend my whole life with me? I'll make no comment on what they said for fear they'll grow angry and never show me their charms again. Anyway, there are only a few of them. Even now, not all of them still echo in my solitude. And those with the fullest sound are not the ones that reach the favored corners. I don't know who silences them or what the secret of their penetration is. I don't know which ones will succeed in reaching, alighting, and falling asleep upon the mysterious objects hidden for who knows how long in the darkest attics. But unknown silences are waiting there to raise anew the stilled sound of their memory.

Always send me words that will last.

Margarita:

I know. You find it strange that I haven't written you for so long. But a long time ago a windy night changed the direction of my despair, bending my anguish to another side. I laughed at myself as if realizing that I'd been walking around with my soul turned inside out, the unfinished edges for others to see and the smooth seams for myself. I looked back over the obscure tracks of my letters and discovered that my hands had been mistaken, both in what they gave and in what they hoped to receive. I'd made a futile effort to deduce a little mystery. And perhaps even that little bit was put there by me. And I suffered a great deal, for although my friends were women of free intelligence and iridescent spirit, they wrote me very little.

But that night, when the wind blew in a different direction, someone in the street called out to my heart. And from within my dream it slipped out towards the world. Only my heart could search for the things that interested me, so after that I never again took an interest in anything, or searched for anything. Not even my heart itself.

Note:

"Mistaken Hands" was published in the *Revista Nacional* of Montevideo in April, 1946, its only publication during Felisberto's lifetime.

THE CROCODILE

ONE AUTUMN NIGHT WHEN IT WAS hot and humid I went to a city that was almost unknown to me; what little light there was in the streets was muted by the humidity and the few leaves left on the trees. I went into a café near a church, sat down at a table in the back and thought about my life. I knew how to isolate the hours of happiness and enclose myself within them. First, with my eyes, I stole anything left carelessly out on the street or inside a house, then I bore it back to my solitude. Going over it in my head gave me such pleasure that if people had known they would have hated me. But there might not be many happy times left to me. I'd once toured cities like this one, giving piano concerts; my hours of pleasure had been few since I lived in the anguish of having to assemble a group of people who wanted to lend their support to a concert. I had to co-ordinate them, influence each one, and try to find an active man among them. It was almost always like having a fight with slow, distracted drunks. Just as I managed to bring one person in, another would slip away. On top of that I had to practice and write my newspaper articles.

But for some time I hadn't had to worry about that anymore, having managed to obtain a position with a large company that sold women's stockings. I figured that stockings were more necessary than concerts and would be easier to market. A friend of mine told the manager that as a concert pianist I had many female contacts and had visited many cities, and could make use of the influence of my concerts to peddle stockings.

The manager pulled a face but hired me. It wasn't only my friend's influence that made him accept me: my advertising slogan for the stockings had won second prize. The brand name was *Illusion*, and my slogan was "Nowadays, who doesn't cherish their Illusions?" But selling stockings also turned out to be very hard, and every day I expected to be called back to headquarters and have my travel allowance cut off. At first, I made a tremendous effort. (Selling stockings had nothing to do with my concerts—the only people I had to negotiate with were shopkeepers.) When I happened to run into old acquaintances, I told them that as the representative of a large company I could travel independently and no longer had to oblige my friends to sponsor concerts when the time was not ripe for them. The time had never been ripe for my concerts. In that very city, they'd made some rather unusual excuses: the Club president, annoyed because I took him away from his card game, told me that someone who had a lot of relatives had just died and half the city was in mourning. This time, I simply announced that I would be spending a few days there, to see if the desire for a concert arose of its own accord. But a concert pianist who sold stockings made a bad impression. As for the stockings, every morning I worked myself up to sell them and every night I was let down: it was like getting dressed and undressed. This constant replenishment of the brute force I needed to keep going at the shopkeepers, who were always very busy, took a lot out of me. But now, resigned to being fired, I was trying to enjoy myself for as long as my travel allowance lasted.

Suddenly I noticed that a blind man with a harp had come into the café; I'd seen him that afternoon. I decided to leave before I lost my will to enjoy life, but as I walked out I saw him again; the brim of his hat was crumpled and his eyes rolled towards the heavens as he struggled to play. A few of the harp's strings had been clumsily repaired, and covering the pale wood of the instrument and the man's whole body was a grime such as I had never seen before. I thought of myself and felt depressed.

When I switched on the light in my hotel room, I saw the bed that was my bed for those few days. The sheets were turned down, and the nickel-plated bars made me think of a young madwoman, yielding herself to every passerby. Once I was in bed I turned the light off but couldn't sleep. I switched it back on. The bulb peeked out from under its shade like an eyeball from beneath a dark lid. I turned it off at once and tried to think about the stocking business, but in the darkness I still saw the lampshade a moment longer. Fading to a lighter color, its shape began shifting to one side, melting into the darkness as if it were the soul of the shade, departing for purgatory. All this happened in the time it would take a blotter to absorb some spilled ink.

The next morning, after dressing and working myself up for the day, I went to see if the night train had brought bad news. There was no letter or telegram for me. I decided to visit every business on one of the main streets. There was a store at the top of the street. Going in, I found myself in a room crammed to the ceiling with trinkets and rags. There was only one naked dummy, made of red cloth with a black knob for a head. I clapped my hands and all the rags instantly swallowed up the sound. From behind the dummy appeared a girl of about ten who said rudely, "What do you want?"

"Is the owner here?"

"There is no owner. My mama's the one in charge."

"She's not here?"

"She went to see Doña Vicenta and she's coming right back."

Then a boy of about three appeared. He clung to his sister's skirt and they stood there a while, all in a row—dummy, girl, boy. "I'll wait," I said.

The girl said nothing. I sat down on a box and started playing with her little brother. Remembering I still had one of the choco-

lates I'd bought at the movies, I dug it out of my pocket. The little
boy quickly came and took it away from me. I covered my face with
my hands and pretended to sob. My eyes were covered, but in the
dark hollow of my hands I opened my fingers a crack and began
watching the boy. He observed me without moving, and I cried
harder and harder. Finally he decided to put the chocolate on my
knee. Then I laughed and gave it to him. At that moment I realized
that my face was wet.

I left before the owner came back. Passing a jewelry shop, I
looked at myself in a mirror and my eyes were dry. After lunch I was
sitting in the café but left immediately when I saw the blind man
with the harp rolling his eyes. Then I walked to a solitary plaza in a
deserted area and sat down on a bench facing a wall covered with
vines. There I thought about the morning's tears. I was intrigued by
the fact that they had come, and I wanted to be alone, as if I'd gone
off to play in secret with the toy I'd accidentally switched on a few
hours earlier. It shamed me a little, in my own eyes, to start crying
for no reason, even if it was only in fun, as it had been that morning.
With some hesitation I wrinkled up my eyes and nose to see if the
tears would arrive, but then thought that I shouldn't just go looking
for tears, like someone wringing out a rag. I'd have to give myself
over to it with real sincerity. I buried my face in my hands. There
was something serious about that position; unexpectedly I was
moved. I felt a kind of pity for myself and the tears began to flow.

I'd been crying for a while when I saw two female legs clad in
semi-sheer *Illusion* stockings climbing down from the top of the
wall. Then I noticed a green skirt that was hard to see against the
vines. I hadn't heard the ladder being set down. The woman was
on the bottom rung and I quickly dried my tears but hung my head
low, as if I were pensive. The woman slowly walked over and sat
next to me. She'd climbed down with her back to me and I didn't
know what her face looked like. Finally she said, "What's wrong?
You can trust me . . ."

A few moments went by. I knotted my brow as if to hide behind it and wait there. I'd never adopted this expression before and my eyebrows were quivering. Then I made a gesture with my hand as if to begin speaking, though what I might say to her had not yet occurred to me. She spoke once more. "Talk to me, just talk. I have children. I know what heartache is."

I'd already imagined a face for that woman and that green skirt. But when she said this about heartache and children, I imagined a different one. At the same time, I said, "I have to think a little bit."

"With this kind of thing, the more you think the worse it gets," she replied.

I thought a wet rag had suddenly fallen nearby. But it turned out to be a large banana leaf, heavy with moisture. After a short pause, she picked up the conversation again, "Tell me the truth. What's she like?"

At first this struck me as funny. Then a girlfriend I once had came into my mind. Whenever I didn't feel like taking a walk with her along a stream—where she'd strolled with her father when he was alive—this girlfriend of mine would weep silently. Then, even though it bored me to be forever going to the same place, I indulged her. Thinking of her, I had the idea of saying to the woman now at my side, "She was a woman who often wept."

This woman placed her hands, which were large and reddish, on her green skirt and told me, laughing, "You men always believe in a woman's tears."

I thought of my own tears, a bit disconcerted. I stood up from the bench and said, "I believe you're mistaken. But thank you for comforting me all the same."

And I left without looking at her.

The next day, late in the morning, I went into one of the largest shops. The owner laid my stockings out on the counter and stroked them for some time with his stumpy fingers. He seemed not to hear my words. His sideburns were shot through with gray, as if he'd left shaving cream on them. Meanwhile, several women came in; before attending to them, he signaled me with one of the fingers that had caressed the stockings that he was not going to buy them. I didn't move and thought about persisting. Maybe later when no one else was around I could start up a conversation with him; I'd tell him about an herb which, when dissolved in water, could dye his sideburns. The women weren't leaving and I felt unusually impatient; I longed to leave that shop, that city, that life. I thought about my country and about many other things. And suddenly, just as I was beginning to calm down, I had an idea. What would happen if I started crying right in front of all these people? It struck me as a very violent thing to do, but I'd been wanting to do something out of the ordinary, to put the world to the test, for a long time. I also needed to prove to myself that I was capable of great violence. And before I could change my mind I sat down in a little chair backed up against the counter and with all those people around me I put my hands to my face and began emitting sobbing noises. Almost simultaneously, a woman let out a loud cry and said, "A man is weeping."

Then I heard a hubbub of voices and snatches of conversation: "Don't go near him, little girl . . ." "Maybe he just heard some bad news . . ." "The train came in only a little while ago, there hasn't been time for the mail . . ." From between my fingers I saw a fat woman saying, "To think how the world is now. If my children couldn't see me, I'd be crying too!" At first the tears didn't come and I was desperate; I was even afraid they'd think I was playing a joke on them and have me arrested. But finally I choked up from my anguish and the tremendous effort I was making, and the first tears were possible. I felt a heavy hand settle on my shoulder and when I heard the owner's voice I recognized the fingers that had stroked the stockings. He said, "But *compañero*, a man's got to have some spirit. . . ."

Then I stood up, as if some mechanism had been activated,

took my two hands away from my face, removed the third one that was on my shoulder, and said, my face still wet, "I'm fine, really. I have lots of spirit! It's just that sometimes this comes over me; it's like a memory. . . ."

Through the expectant silence that fell around my words, I heard a woman say, "Ay! He's weeping over a memory. . . ."

"That's all for now, señoras," the owner announced.

I smiled and dried my face off. Then the knot of people that had formed began milling around and a small woman with mad eyes appeared and said, "I know you. I think I've seen you somewhere else, when you were agitated."

I thought she must have seen me in a concert, flinging myself around during the finale, but I kept my mouth shut. Conversation broke out among the women and some began to leave. The one who recognized me stayed there with me. Another one came over and said, "I know you sell stockings. By chance, some friends and I. . . ."

The owner intervened. "Don't worry, señora," he said, adding (to me), "Come back this afternoon."

"I'm leaving town after lunch. Do you want two dozen?"

"No, half a dozen should be. . . ."

"A dozen is the minimum order the company will accept. . . ."

Without going any closer to the owner, I took out my sales book and began filling in the order form, writing against a glass door, and surrounded by women talking loudly. I was afraid the owner would change his mind. Finally he signed the order and I went outside with everyone else.

Word soon got out that I had "this thing" that would come over me, which at first was like a memory. I wept in other stores and sold more stockings than usual. By the time I'd wept in several cities, my sales figures were comparable to any other salesman's.

Once they called me to company headquarters—I'd wept my way across the entire north of the country at that point—and as I was waiting my turn to speak to the manager I could hear another travelling salesman saying in the next room, "I do all I can, but I'm not going to start crying just so they'll buy from me!"

And the sickly voice of the manager replied, "You've got to do whatever it takes, even cry for them. . . ."

The salesman interrupted, "But I can't get the tears to come!"

After a silence, the manager said, "What? Who told you about that?"

"Yes! There's one guy who gushes tears. . . ."

The sickly voice began laughing with some difficulty, between bouts of coughing. Then I heard mumbling and footsteps moving away.

After a while, they called me in and had me cry in front of the manager, the supervisors, and all the other employees. When the manager first had me come in and the situation was explained, he laughed painfully until tears came to his eyes. He asked me, in the most courteous way, for a demonstration. Hardly had I accepted when a number of employees who'd been waiting outside the door came in. There was a lot of commotion and they asked me not to cry yet. "Hurry up! One of the travelling salesmen is going to cry," I heard someone say from behind a screen.

"But why?"

"How should I know!"

I was sitting beside the manager at his big desk; they had phoned one of the company's owners but he couldn't come. The men weren't quieting down, and one shouted out, "Think of your sweet mama, that'll make you cry!"

"When they stop talking, I'll cry," I told the manager.

He threatened them in his sickly voice, and after a few moments of relative silence I looked out a window at the crown of a tree—we were on the second floor—buried my face in my hands and tried to cry. I was a little dismayed. Whenever I'd cried before, the people around me hadn't been aware of my real feelings, but these men knew I was going to cry and that inhibited me. When the tears finally came, I took one hand away from my face, both to get my handkerchief out and so they could see that my face was wet. Some laughed and others looked serious; then I shook my face violently and they all laughed. But then they were silent until they began to laugh again. I wiped my tears away as the sickly voice repeated, "Very good, very good." Maybe they were all disappointed. And I felt like an empty bottle, still dripping. I wanted to react; I was in a bad mood and felt like behaving badly. Catching up to the manager, I said, "I don't want any of the others using the same technique to sell stockings. I want the company to acknowledge my . . . my initiative and grant me a certain period of exclusivity."

"Come back tomorrow and we'll talk about it."

The next day the secretary had the document already drawn up and read it aloud: "The company hereby pledges to refrain from using, and to enforce respect for, the system of advertising which consists of weeping. . . ." Then they both laughed and the manager said that was no good. While he edited the document, I strolled out to the front desk. Behind it was a girl who watched me as she talked to me; her eyes looked as if they were painted on from the inside.

"So you cry because you like crying?"

"Yes."

"Then I know more than you do—you don't even know you have a sorrow of some kind."

I was pensive a moment, then said, "Look: I may not be the happiest person around, but I know how to make do with my misfortune. I'm almost lucky."

As I walked away—the manager was calling me—I stole a look at her gaze: she'd placed it on me, as if laying a hand on my shoulder.

On my next sales trip, I was in a small city. It was a sad day and I didn't feel like crying. I'd rather have been alone in my room, listening to the rain and thinking how the water was separating me from everyone. I travelled hidden behind a mask painted with tears, but my face was tired.

Suddenly I noticed that someone had approached me and was asking, "What's wrong?"

Then, like an employee caught in a moment of idleness, I felt I had to go back to my task. Putting my hands over my face I began making sobs.

That year I cried until December, stopped crying for January and part of February, and started crying again after Carnival. The break did me good and I went back to crying with renewed vigor—I'd missed the success my weeping brought. A certain pride in crying had been born within me. There were a lot of salesmen around. But I was an actor who could inhabit his role on the spur of the moment, convincing the public with his tears. . . .

That year, I starting weeping in the west and reached a city where my concerts had been successful. The second time I played there, the public had greeted me with a long, affectionate ovation; I thanked them, standing next to the piano, and they wouldn't let me sit down to begin the concert. This time I would undoubtedly be giving at least a brief recital. The first time I wept there, I was in the most luxurious hotel, at lunchtime on a radiant day. I'd eaten and had a cup of coffee, when, elbows on the table, I covered my face with my hands. A few moments later, some friends I'd just greeted came over; I let them stand there, and meanwhile a poor old woman—I don't know where she came from—sat down at my table and I watched her from between my fingers which were already wet. She lowered her head and said nothing, but she had a face so sad it made you feel like bursting into tears. . . .

The day I gave my concert I was feeling a nervousness brought on by fatigue. As I played the last piece in the first half of the program, I took one of the movements too fast. I tried to slow down but grew clumsy and didn't have sufficient balance or strength; all I could do was go on, but my hands were getting tired, I was losing clarity and I realized I wasn't going to make it to the finale. Then, before I could think, I'd taken my hands from the keyboard and put them on my face. It was the first time I wept onstage.

There were murmurs of surprise, and someone, I don't know why, tried to applaud, but other people were mumbling and I stood up. I covered my eyes with one hand, and groping along the piano with the other I tried to walk offstage. A few women cried out, thinking I was about to fall into the orchestra pit. I was halfway through a door in the wing when someone shouted from the upper tier, "Crooo-co-diiiiile!"

I heard laughter, but went to the dressing room, washed my face, reappeared immediately and finished the first part of the program with fresh, clean hands. Afterwards, many people came to say hello to me and the cry of "crocodile" sparked much comment. "It seems to me that the person who shouted that is correct," I said. "I really don't know why I cry; weeping comes over me and I can't do anything about it. It may be as natural for me as it is for the crocodile. After all, I don't know why the crocodile weeps, either."

One of the people I'd just been introduced to had a long face, and since his hair was cut short and stood on end, his head looked like a brush. Another person in the circle pointed him out and told me, "Our friend here is a doctor. What do you say, doctor?"

I blanched. He looked at me with a police detective's eyes and asked, "Tell me one thing: do you cry more by day or by night?"

I remembered that I never cried at night because I never went out selling at night, and answered, "I cry only in the daytime."

I don't remember his other questions. But in the end he advised me, "Don't eat any meat. Your system has been poisoned for a long time."

A few days later a party was thrown for me at the town's finest club. I rented a dress coat with an immaculate white vest and when I looked at myself in the mirror I thought, "Well, they can't say this crocodile doesn't have a fine white belly. Why, I believe that beast even has a double chin, just like mine—and it's voracious, too. . . ."

Not many people were at the club when I got there, and I realized I'd arrived too early. I saw a gentleman from the committee and told him I would like to work a little at the piano. That way I'd have a pretext for my early arrival. We went through a green curtain and I found myself in a large, empty hall set up for dancing. Opposite the curtain, at the other end, was the piano. The gentleman from the committee and the porter walked me over, and as they were opening the piano, the gentleman—he had black eyebrows and white hair— told me that the party would be a great success, and that the head of the literary society, a friend of mine, would give a very lovely speech, which he had heard. He tried to recall a few phrases but then decided it was best not to tell me anything about it. I put my hands on the piano and they left. As I played, I thought, "Tonight I won't cry . . . that would be very ugly . . . the head of the literary society may want me to weep as evidence of the success of his speech. But I won't cry for anything in the world."

For a while I'd noticed the green curtain moving, and suddenly a tall girl emerged from among its folds, her hair hanging loose; her eyes were narrowed, as if to see across a distance. She was looking at me, and came towards me, carrying something in one hand; behind her appeared a maid who caught up with her and began speaking in her ear. I took the opportunity to look at her legs and realized she had only one stocking on. She kept gesturing to indicate that the conversation was over, but the maid went on talking and the two of them returned to their subject as if to a tempting delicacy. Still playing the piano while they conversed, I had time to think "What can she want with the stocking . . . ? Was there some problem with it . . . and knowing that I represent the company—and right now, during a party!"

Finally she came over and said, "Excuse me, I'd like you to autograph a stocking."

At first I laughed; then I tried to react as if the request had been made of me before. I began explaining why the stocking wouldn't hold up under a pen; on other occasions I'd solved that problem by signing a label which the woman in question then glued to her stocking. But in giving these explanations, I displayed the experience of a former dry-goods salesman who later became a pianist.

Anguish was stealing over me when she sat down on the piano bench and said, as she put the stocking on, "It's too bad you're such a liar . . . you should have thanked me for the idea."

I had placed my eyes on her legs. Then I took them away and my thoughts became embroiled. There was a displeased silence. She bent her head and let her hair fall forward, and beneath that blonde curtain her hands moved as if they were fleeing. I said nothing, and she took forever. Finally, the leg made a dancing movement, and as she stood up, the foot, its toes pointed, slipped on the shoe; the hands pulled back the hair, and waving at me silently she left.

When people started coming in, I went to the bar. It occurred to me to order a whisky. The bartender named all the different brands and since I didn't know any of them I said, "Give me that last one."

I climbed onto a bar stool, trying not to wrinkle the tails of my dress coat. I must have looked more like a black parrot than a crocodile. I was silent, thinking about the girl with the stocking; the memory of her busy hands was disturbing.

I felt myself guided into the auditorium by the head of the literary society. The dance stopped for a moment and he gave his speech. Several times he uttered the words "vicissitudes" and "necessity." When they applauded, I raised my arms like an orchestra conductor about to "attack" and once they were silent I said, "Now that I should be crying, I can't. I can't speak, either, and I don't want to keep apart any longer the couples who will now join together to dance." I concluded with a bow.

I turned around to embrace the man from the literary society and saw the girl with the stocking over his shoulder. Smiling at me, she raised the left side of her skirt a little to show me the place on her stocking where she'd pasted a small portrait of me cut out of the program. I smiled, full of gladness, but then blurted out a piece of idiocy which everyone repeated, "Very good, very good: the leg of the heart."

And yet I felt fortunate, and went to the bar. I climbed onto a stool again and the bartender asked me, "White Horse Whisky?"

And I answered, with the gesture of a musketeer drawing his sword, "White Horse or Black Parrot."

In a short while a boy walked over with one hand hidden behind his back.

"Chubby told me it doesn't bother you when they call you 'Crocodile.'"

"That's true. I like it."

Then, taking his hand from behind his back, he showed me a caricature of a big crocodile that looked a lot like me; it had one small hand in its mouth, where its teeth were a keyboard, and from the other hand dangled a stocking it was using to wipe away its tears.

When my friends took me back to my hotel I thought about all the weeping I'd done in that country and took malevolent pleasure in having deceived them; I considered myself a bourgeois of anguish. But when I was alone in my room, something unexpected happened. First I looked at myself in the mirror; I had the caricature in my hand and started looking at the crocodile and at my own face, in succession. Suddenly, though I had no intention of imitating the crocodile, my face began to weep, all on its own. I watched, as if I were looking at a sister whose unhappiness I knew nothing about. My face had new wrinkles and the tears trickled across them. I turned off the light and lay down. My face went on weeping; the tears slid along my nose and onto the pillow. I fell asleep like that. When I woke up I felt the prickle of dried tears. I wanted to get out of bed and wash my eyes, but I was afraid my face would start crying again. I lay still, rolling my eyes in the dark, like that blind man who played the harp.

Note:

"The Crocodile" first appeared in the Montevideo magazine *Marcha* in December, 1949. In 1962, it was published as a 55-page illustrated book by Ediciones del Este.

THE NEW HOUSE

for Esterlina Vignart

FOR A WHILE NOW I'VE BEEN jotting down shorthand symbols in front of a friend who's across a café table from me. I've asked him to forgive me, explaining that I have to make some notes. He won't take it badly. He always expects me to do something that's somehow remote from reality. What I truly want is to give my eyes a rest—writing is less tiring to them—along with my face, and my soul. If I weren't writing I'd have to display a smile or a gesture to my friend, and say some words that fit in with his idea of me, which it suits me for him to keep. He thinks that although I have only a little money left, it doesn't really worry me; I'm an artist who lives "on a mountain in the moon," as he puts it, and only descends at odd moments, full of good grace and forgiveness for this small city where it turns out to be so difficult to hold even a single piano concert. He doesn't believe I experience earthly anguish, so he tells me with an incredible wealth of detail about all the failures he's met with in trying to finance this concert. But not only am I here on earth, thinking about how I'll pay the hotel and the bus to take me away from this place, I'm flat on the ground. Since it costs me a great deal to get up and reach the high places his illusions assign me, I'd rather turn my face and eyes toward this paper, misleading my friend with this flight of signs. He says I have to try to react. I'm bored with this; I think that if I let myself drop to the

very bottom of my sadness I might be able to react better afterwards. I must give myself over now to foreseeing the worst. Perhaps I'll have to wash dishes or work as a laborer and ruin my
hands. I know how to type a little, but once they see me fall so low
people may write me off entirely, and think that I play the piano as
badly as I type. They'll say that if those who once admired me as a
pianist could see my typing tests, they would discover, glancing
over the written pages, that they understood nothing about the
piano and that in all likelihood I was just as bad a pianist as a typist.
Then, their minds closed against me, they wouldn't listen to the
explanation that I've studied the piano since I was a child but have
only been typing for a short time. I wouldn't be able to compete
with any speed at shorthand, either, nor can I think of anyone who
might need shorthand in this slow city that I must leave at all costs
but where I would so much like to stay.

I had to stop writing for a while; my eyes were escaping out to the
street where a fine, greenish sand shimmered in the summer sun;
they were also straying over to the shade of the orange trees that line
the sidewalks. But I had to bring them quickly back to my friend's
face because when he saw I wasn't writing he began telling me about
the concert again. It pains me to think that there are people as generous as this man, who has done so much for me—and also to think
how far I am from being a person like that. He himself must have
caused the last pesos the city council had earmarked for cultural
events to evaporate; he told me that a week earlier a girl singer had
given a concert that was very bad and disagreeable and caused great
suffering to the audience, but the singer was travelling with her
mother and they had to be saved. As a result, the mayor had said
there would be no more city council money for concerts this year.

My eyes had climbed all the way up to the tiles of the old sloping
roofs on some of the houses. To cover over the part about the mayor
and make conversation with my friend, I asked him what era those
houses dated from. He couldn't tell me, but immediately began re-

peating the story of the School Inspector's transfer, which was why the Department of Inspection couldn't pay for a children's concert. And with the same sadness, still awaiting some mysterious change in my situation, I thought that from those old houses had come the people who built the other, newer ones, with roofs that couldn't be seen, which looked like the daughters of the older ones except that those now had the warmth conferred by the long passage of time, especially compared to one unpleasant new house which I tried to blame for the fact that things were going badly for me—modern people must live there, the kind of people who were interested in such false forms of culture. This new house had torn the orange trees from its sidewalk the better to show off some disproportionately large blocks stuck on its facade. What was more, it gave off a strident white light, first attracting the eyes and then violently repelling them. It even kept the neighboring houses from being seen. (A few summers before, I'd made contact with one of those houses.)

My friend suddenly noticed that I had departed—for the moon, according to him—and left him with my face which probably lacked all expression, like the suit we leave hanging over a chair while we sleep. When he "saw" me come back again he returned to the subject of the concert and this time could not abandon it until a moment of vexation had occurred, which he sidestepped with great dignity. He then rose from his chair, begging me to forgive him and give him another chance to work out my situation. The vexation began with the information that an Educational Development Committee with a lot of money could have given a concert for the children but had used up all its money on dental services for them instead. Then came the disappointment of the clubs: one had spent everything on a party and another didn't even have the money for a party. Then he told me that a while ago several members of two of the clubs had formed a group of contributors for special events, but that even "those fellows" had been "burned" by the misuse of their funds. And last came the thing I already knew best: that a concert could not be financed by ticket sales alone; there was neither the time to sell tickets nor anyone who would commit to selling them and, even in the best of cases, the sales wouldn't cover the costs.

I don't quite know why, but when he started talking about the contributors already burned by misuse, a certain uncontrollable reaction was sparked in the depths of my anguish. Then I began saying things that my friend would interrupt.

"Please, for the rest of our conversation, let's talk about something more pleasant." (I might be taken to the police station for failing to pay.)

"Here are some—"

"In any case, I shall depart proud in the knowledge that I have a friend. . . ."

"Wait a minute, let me—"

"I'll come back just to spend the summer. . . ."

It was then, already up out of his seat and looking at the street, that he asked me—his pair of very old hands with very long nails that were very black around the edges resting on the table—to forgive him and give him one last chance.

"You don't have to make this sacrifice. My dear friend, it humiliates me even more," I went so far as to shout at him, almost.

I was left alone in a state of unbelievable mortification. I didn't want to be indebted to that dignified stance of his, in which he seemed to be grasping at the final reserves of his being. As I thought of the means he might resort to, I grew alarmed. Also, abandoning myself to some new hope that he might save me seemed ignoble. I didn't want him to lose the illusion that I was worthy of him. For my own self-respect, I didn't want him to be aware of my fear of this situation, even if he were to discover later that I was concealing my fear. I knew he would appreciate the fact that I wasn't letting my "ragged underwear" show, as he'd once said of someone else. On the one hand, it suited me to be seen in a light that would encourage him to find a way out of the situation, since there was no other solution and he had so generously offered to try, but on the other hand I seemed to be making use of him for my own benefit to a shameful degree. It did very little good to swear to myself that I would later send him a handsome gift. And, too, my disappointment that my piano aroused such scant desire to hear it, to the point that my poor friend had to make such sacrifices, pained me greatly.

Finally I found myself gazing in hatred at the new house. But once I was calmer, and almost resigned to giving in and being a little ignoble and losing some of my sense of shame, I thought I shouldn't allow my eyes to know and nurture hatred, just as innocent children shouldn't be allowed to. And I discovered that I shouldn't taint other innocents—my memories of one of the houses—with hatred, either.

A few years earlier, I'd awoken in a room in a country inn to discover that our thoughts are produced in a region of our innermost being marked by the quality of silence. Even amid a great city's most strident clamor we think in silence about where we're going or what we have to do, or whatever it is that corresponds to our desires. And the silence in which our feelings take shape is still deeper. We feel love in silence, before the thoughts come, and then the words, and then the acts, always moving farther towards the outside, towards the noise. Some thoughts can hide within silence and never become words, though they may carry out hidden acts. But there are also feelings that hide in silence behind deceptive thoughts. The silence where feelings and thoughts are formed is the place where the style of a human being's life and life work is formed.

Since that night in that dark room in a country inn, I find pleasure in discovering the extremely diverse and contradictory thoughts and feelings that exist not only in different people but within a single human being. Perhaps it's because of this that the friend who is defending me now once felt my understanding during a period when this whole city was criticizing him. The story about one of the houses that I have yet to tell is due to it, as well.

A few hours after arriving in this city for the first time, I met this friend. Soon he'd organized an event for the poet who accompanied me on that tour and myself. (We performed poetic and musical numbers as part of a single show.) A few days later, our friend's mother died. When we brought him home from the cemetery he was limp as a rag. He wept on and off, like an intermittent rain. After the poet, whom all of us greatly admired and loved, had left, he wept for a long time without stopping, then fell into a deep sleep. Then everyone else left, too. The only ones still there were an old Indian woman, sleeping in another room, and me, sitting in a very comfortable chair where I, too, fell asleep. That happened as night was falling, and he woke up at about ten p.m. As a very special favor, he asked me to go and find an individual in the café on the corner. When I brought him that person, my friend said, without giving me the chance to leave the two of them alone, "Tomorrow, without fail, put thirty pesos on it." I accompanied the man who'd taken the wager to the door, and he told me, "He's crazy. That's the number on his mother's cross in the cemetery." Then he told everyone.

The consequences for my friend were terrible. Not only because the number wasn't drawn and he lost the thirty pesos, which was a lot of money then, but because he was accused of sacrilege, of trying to profit from his mother's death; people talked about "thirty pieces of silver" and concluded that he hadn't loved his mother at all.

Here I intervened, pointing out that it was possible for virtues and defects to dwell together in the same person. I had many examples because this was "my game." Just as my friend was always attentive to the appearance of any number, I was attentive to the appearance of feelings, thoughts, actions, or any part of reality that might jar our preconceived ideas about it. A little bored by now with observing all this in myself, I also wanted to understand the things produced in the intimate silence of others when—intentionally or unintentionally—they displayed them, and the things that might then happen within the free play of circumstances. Indeed, I'd already found something to interest me in the fact that my friend loved his mother and had a passion for gambling, and that the fault people found with him was based on the idea that if he were a gambler he couldn't love his mother. But further surprises, which I would encounter in myself and in others, were still in store for me in that city.

The event the poet and I staged was a success. He spoke about Granada, for example—this was one of our numbers—conjuring the orgy of water the Arabs had created in the Alhambra to make up for what they lacked in the desert; he spoke of the moon as a burnished scimitar, and before his words had come to an end he turned to me and I began playing "Granada," the serenade by Albéniz. Though both numbers were of interest and referred to the same city, the mystery, the medium, and the "silence" from which each emerged was different, as literature and the cinema are different even when they have the same plot and make the same logical connections. But the people who attended this performance enjoyed the idea of this external coordination between poetry and music, and must have thought they were thus amassing a greater quantity of knowledge about Granada. They neither spoke nor applauded during those moments—we performed the two numbers without interruption—and it charmed me to see them given over to their "silence." When, in passing from literature to music, they all turned their heads the other way, they looked like sleepers changing position.

Their bearing, even when they came to congratulate us afterwards, was so touching it made us think that our performance had not been as good as their attitude, and that in reality we were deceiving them.

Among the last to leave were a gentleman and his daughter, who invited us to visit them the next day. This gentleman bore a strong resemblance to Einstein. He, too, had an almost white mane of bushy hair that stuck up from his head like a ranch's wattle fence. His tie was a soft bow that drooped like a dog's ears. He hardly spoke at all; he kept the books for some large businesses and had some position on the city council, I didn't know what it was, but according to him and his daughter he was a poet. She spoke of the successes she'd had as a reciter of poetry, and said vulgar things with false emotion. She talked continually and that was fine with me since it concealed the fact that I couldn't take my eyes off of her. I was trying to detach her from her words, like someone extracting a sweet from infinite layers of cardboard, paper, string, frills, and other nuisances.

The next day we went to visit them in one of the houses with tiled roofs that I was looking at now. We walked into a portico filled with plants and a little parlor full of knickknacks which, draped in the afternoon's last, dusty sunlight, seemed doubly fragile and hazy. I was afraid of stepping on a black cat under my chair, and of making some gesture that would knock against a small table with fragile legs where another cat sat. This one was white, carved out of bone, and if it fell it would bring down other knickknacks with it. Nevertheless, the reciter of poetry made all sorts of movements with enviable confidence: she even allowed herself to lower her eyelids. I told my poet friend that when she had her eyes like that her stance was somewhere between infinity and a sneeze. But she was divine, and I found all my feelings tied in knots. She recited poems by her father, who bowed his head when we praised his beautiful sonnets. I raised mine to his daughter and her eyelids fell lower and lower as she looked at me.

Now, a few years later, I found my own eyelids lowered over

these memories, and also from the anguish of being unable to pay for the hotel and the bus. But unexpected angels still exist, and beat their wings. My friend arrived, beating his arms in the air and reproaching me for not having told him that the mayor was such a good friend of mine that he would use money earmarked for something else; I was to meet them there that night, in that very café.

That night I found only my friend. But he told me, "No, he says we should go to his house." A few steps away he raised an index finger—he could easily have been doing so to point out my errors, which he was well acquainted with—and rang the bell of the new house. We entered a courtyard as desolate as a chipped coffeepot. Then we were led into a parlor with fragile tables and the cat carved from bone. At last the poet appeared and when I asked him if things were going well, he replied, "This morning, when my daughter was knotting my tie for me"—the bow tie that drooped like a dog's ears—"she told me, 'Father, you are a great poet, you have a high position in society and a new house.'"

Note:

"The New House" was published in Montevideo in 1959 in the *State Insurance Bank Almanac* (*Almanaque del Banco de Seguros del Estado*).

LANDS OF MEMORY

I'M TEMPTED TO BELIEVE THAT my first acquaintance with life began at nine o'clock one morning on a train. I was twenty-three years old. My father had gone with me to the station and as I was boarding the train a stranger came over to greet us and asked me, "You're the pianist?"

"That's right."

"I figured it out from the way you look. I'm the 'Mandolión.'" That was his way of pronouncing "bandoneon."

As we vaguely took in his explanations, my father—who was a little slower than I was—stared at him through his glasses, which made his eyes look bigger; he also had his mouth open and was about to tell him something, but the whistle blew and he only had time to give me a quick embrace.

The Mandolión slowly lowered his body, grown fat inside his tough, sallow skin, onto the seat; he looked bloated, like a dead animal. At his waist, where the pants ended and the jacket began, his white shirt spilled over on all sides as if he were wearing a life preserver.

He began telling me about the "Violin." The Violin lived in the city we were headed for and had found us the job there.

I wondered what my father might have wanted to say to the Mandolión; it probably involved some sort of promise to protect me. But

I couldn't imagine reaching any type of understanding with this young animal, who would never let an idea emerge except on condition that it make an about-face and return with something to fatten him up even more. He might have fobbed my father off, saying "Sure, don't worry" and pursing his lips to make room for a cigarette, but then he'd have gone right back to talking about the Violin. His current idea—it seemed to have settled into the corneas of his large eyes, which were placid as an ox's—was waiting for the moment he would first meet the violinist; the idea would then perch nearby and wait for the Violin to speak to the owner of the café where we were going to play. And the idea would sit there next to the owner for three months—the duration of the contract—trying all the while to convince the boss to extend the contract and raise our salary.

At the beginning of the conversation I'd been careful not to let him see the flimsy, stretching filaments of molasses that were my emotions as I slowly detached myself from Montevideo. I was sick with anguish, with the sound of the train and the gray of the houses that our speed turned into stripes on the windowpane, and with the thought of what I was leaving behind in Montevideo: my wife, in the middle of a weighty expectancy.

One of the Mandolión's feet had ruptured the laces of a shabby yellow ankle boot with its tongue sticking out. The foot was resting on top of the case for the "mandolión" (instrument). Suddenly the foot removed itself from the case and the Mandolión (man) took out the "mandolión" (instrument) and began to play.

We were traveling first class and I didn't want to look at the other passengers' faces. The Mandolión was lamenting that the owner of the café hadn't sent the cost of the fare, rather than the tickets, to the Pianists' Association, where we'd been hired for the job. He would have taken a second-class ticket and pocketed the difference. I, too, wished for that, because then he wouldn't be playing his bandoneon in first class.

After a while he asked me if I knew anything about the "mandolión." Then he wanted to teach me: "A few notes as you close it, and then, as you're opening it, a few more." I had to tell him I was feeling sick. Fortunately those hands began putting everything away again. They looked like gloves made of human skin and packed so tightly with flesh that the fingers stuck out in all directions. Their capacity for movement was extremely meager; they made only those movements that were indispensable, taking the shortest route and the longest possible time. As they were preparing the "mandolión" to be stowed away, the fingers seemed slow, hard, and stumpy against the inlay of pearly flowers and figures on the instrument's black wood. Before closing the lid of the case, the hands covered the "mandolión" with a cloth that was also black and also strewn with crocheted flowers and figures. Perhaps the instrument was the great luxury of his life and it pleased him to see it covered in flowers. Perhaps, after abandoning himself to this pleasure, he felt the embarrassment that delicate things inspire in this sort of brute; perhaps the word "fancy" formed in his head, and if a buddy happened to be present he would think "women's things"; perhaps, growing ironical and with a bit of a smile on the lips that surrounded his cigarette like a garland, he would try to use those fingers of his to make a gesture indicating something silly and trivial. He would imagine that his fingers had undulated, but in fact they would barely have made a kind of clumsy fluctuation, as if they were solid blocks; if those fingers ever picked up a pencil they probably sweated from the effort of wielding it, and formed numbers and letters that were repellent.

Even though I didn't want him to, the creature I had before me—only half a yard away—would go on existing for the eight hours the journey was going to last. I had the deficiency or weakness of being entirely unable to isolate myself from the people around me. I couldn't forego the task of imagining what anyone near me might be thinking. They, and their way of experiencing their lives, were entering a little into mine, and the sensation of the moments I spent in their vicinity depended on what kind of people they were. This meant that seated as I was across from the Mandolión I couldn't give myself over to thinking whatever I wanted. I had two other irritations, as well: first, I would have preferred death to having him discover my thoughts in my acquiescent face, and second, I would have to defend my face as if it were a naked, sleeping woman. And what was more—as I thought about the nature of that brute—my modesty would seem feminine, and his brutality masculine.

A memory from my childhood stirred as the train crossed Calle Capurro. But the Mandolión was speaking to me just then and the memory was extinguished. After a while, I felt uneasy, as if I'd failed to do something, and I soon realized that the childhood memory from Calle Capurro was tugging at my sleeve to attract my attention once more. The white bars of the railroad crossing I'd just seen weren't the same, and the vine-covered wooden guardhouse where, like a family of spiders, the black switchman had once lived with all his brood, was no longer there. (Once the black man lowered the bars before the streetcar had gone across, trapping it in the railway crossing just as the train was coming. The conductor went full speed ahead and broke through the bars, and some of the passengers, in the emotion of being saved, embraced the conductor and gave him money.)

When I was twelve I walked past there every day and, a few yards from the tracks, entered the home of two French ladies who were teachers. But before crossing the tracks I liked to stop and look off down the rails; the four rails of the two tracks made a very slight curve before they disappeared behind a hill. And the rails would spend all their time waiting, with their backs to the sun, for the monstrous egotists in the train—always riding along thinking about the direction they were heading in—to go over them. Then the rails would bask once more in the admiration of all the grasses that dwelled so peaceably around them.

The two French teachers were sisters, and orphans; they'd come to Montevideo when they were young. They ran a public school and gave private lessons, as well. In their house I was surrounded by girls who were studying to be teachers. The younger sister had a greatly beloved way of swaying her tall body to and fro, and her way of being plump was careless and full of warmth. When her feet brought her body over to my chair and she forced me to look at her by gently hooking a finger under my chin and raising my head, my eyes would gaze up at her as if she were a cathedral, and when she let my head fall so I could reflect upon the homework I hadn't done, my eyes would have a close view of the weave of her gray skirt covering the hidden mountain of her abdomen. The Younger One was almost young. I'd heard it said that she couldn't have a sweetheart because the older sister would throw herself down a well. The Older One always spoke in a very low voice, but other people had to speak to her very loudly; she would cup her hand behind her ear, lean far forward and wrinkle up her whole face as if in deep anguish—listening seemed to cause her pain. Her voice was a trickle that took a long time to reach the surface, as if she were drawing it up from a well with a pump. The person listening to her also had to make an effort; you could hear the thin voice choking before it emerged. Then, while she was talking, you could excuse the little drops of saliva that escaped from her mouth.

Whenever I found the Older One in the front courtyard as I entered that house, it was as if a part of the back of the house had somehow come into the front. If the Older One arrived and started pumping out her thin voice while I was talking to the Younger One, I thought of the depths of that family's past. If the Older One crossed through a sunny spot, I felt that a dark corner of the house and the past was unwittingly crossing through the light.

That house had two backyards. A portico led into the front courtyard, and then a covered walkway led to a second courtyard, which was the first backyard and was surrounded by another arched walkway. Many silent, blind plants lived in that courtyard, but in summer they would stir; I watched them probing the air and they made me smile. From that second courtyard the second backyard could be seen, full of high weeds and low trees. The two backyards were separated by a wire fence and a rickety little gate. To open it, you had to give it many quick shoves; it seemed to take short steps, dragging itself along the ground. One day a little girl who must have been about my age broke it. She'd had to open it quickly because I was chasing her. The girl was being raised by the two teachers. The teachers weren't there, and I was supposed to wait for them. They didn't come, so I had a lot of time to run after my playmate through that solitary house. But while we were running among the high weeds and low trees I fell and got a green stain on one leg of my pants, which were white. I washed the stain with soap, but had trouble rubbing the spot since I was still wearing the pants. Then, to hide the stain and my effort at laundering it, my playmate applied starch and white pigment to me. At home, they looked at the lump it made and laughed, but didn't say anything.

On the left side of the first backyard was the door through which the Older One almost always appeared. When it was closed and I knew there was no one behind it—as on the afternoon when I was chasing my companion—the door mattered very little. But when it was closed and I knew the Older One was in that room, I was also aware that the door wore a different expression. It was like the immobile face of a head that is thinking; it has thoughts inside it, but you don't know what kind of thoughts. Sometimes I could hear her footsteps muttering across that room; perhaps she was getting dressed. And if, through the half-open door, I saw a ripple of white cloth going past or a patch of bare shoulder it made me remember her half-open mouth at the moments when her teeth and the drops of saliva glistened.

A small room at the front of the house which opened onto the front courtyard was the study. Two desks and two bookcases filled it. I didn't like the fact that the Younger One was the mistress of those two desks, which were things for serious men. I forgave her for being in charge, but not for having those desks. I've never met a person who took charge more charmingly. No sooner had she grown angry or said something in agitation than she went red, choking back her words, and swelling with the most responsible prudence, and, so that no aspect of her person would be incorrect, she would lift her right hand to an opening she always had in the right side of her gray skirt. Her fingers were its only fasteners and if she took them away the white strip of her petticoat would declare itself once more where the gray skirt gapped open.

In the room with the desks, the Younger One gave lessons to a blonde young lady whose head always tilted forward; she was the first person whose corneas attracted my attention. Hers were very different from the Mandolión's, which looked as if they were befouled by nicotine and threads of tobacco. His irises looked dirty, too, as if a number of dark colors had been churned up in them. The corneas of the blonde young lady were like newly purchased terrestrial globes, and it was a pleasure to look at the blue country of the iris with its capital city, a very large pupil, in the middle. Once when I was very close to her pupils I saw a table lamp reflected in them—its bulb, incidentally, was held aloft by a naked woman made of bronze. I didn't know whether that young lady's frailty was an affectation or the result of some illness. She had very long fingernails and moved her hands as if she were afraid they would start to hurt. The sensitive protuberances of her fingertips appeared to know that they would be the first to touch any surface, and seemed as delicate her corneas. When the fingers landed on the green of a piece of blotting paper that lay on the desk, they alit at an angle and the fingertips remained hidden below the nails for some time.

Once this young lady was practicing teaching a lesson that explained how a bedroom should be arranged; she said there should be a pair of slippers beside the double bed. She and the teacher looked at each other and smiled, and I remained intrigued by that for a long while.

In one part of the second courtyard (the first backyard) was a round table around which the disciples, all of them girls older than me, would crowd. Sitting in an armchair, the Younger One taught the class. There was one girl dressed in mourning who wore no face powder and was very daring; she recited the lesson with one elbow on the table and her hand to her face. Whenever she didn't remember the lesson she put her hand to her forehead, as if she had a headache, and lowered her eyes to make her gaze fall on her skirt where we knew she was holding an open book. One afternoon the teacher told her not to look at the book. I was scared. The girl denied everything. The teacher told her to stand up. The girl obeyed instantly, spreading her arms out wide to demonstrate that she had no book. Nothing could be heard falling to the floor, either. We were all mystified. Then the little girl who must have been about my age appeared in the kitchen door pricking her nose with a fork. The teacher had to leave the room for a moment and another girl—one who powdered herself so heavily that the hairs of her little moustache stood out against all that powder like pine trees on a sand dune; she was from El Cerro; a bull charged her once and in order to race away she'd had to hitch her narrow skirt up around her waist—asked the one with the book how she'd done it and she explained. As she stood up, she'd closed the book and squeezed it between her thighs; the teacher couldn't see it from the other side of the table. The girl who was my age was still pricking herself with the fork's tiny fingers, as if she were dividing her nose into quarters for us.

One day when the afternoon had just begun, I was crossing the train tracks and a little black boy, the switchman's son, waylaid me.

He often got into fights, and with the sixth sense of the streets he'd realized I was afraid of him. That afternoon he jumped me: all I could do was put my satchel up as a shield and dash towards the teachers' house.

During class, I began suffering over the arithmetic exercises; it was a subject I never knew much about. The Younger One was listening to me repeat the lesson and her bare arms were resting on those of her armchair. I was explaining, "After a tenth comes an eleventh, a twelfth, a thirteenth"—I knew very little, so I stretched out the examples—"a fourteenth . . ."—and just as the teacher asked "Up to what number?" I added, "And so on in succession."

Someone knocked at the door. The teacher went out with her fingers holding the gap in her skirt shut. She spoke in some agitation, with the front door ajar. I caught sight of a policeman's helmet and thought about the little black boy on the railroad tracks, but since I'd raced away I had the only peace of mind a coward can have: that of not having done a thing to his aggressor. I heard the teacher say in a loud voice, "The idea! I won't permit it. He's from a very good family." She came back completely flushed and without her fingers on her skirt.

"What happened with the little black boy?"

"He wanted to hit me . . . my mama always tells me not to fight . . . and then I came running here."

I was tormented. I would so greatly have wished to be brave.

"How dare you lie to me!"

"It's true, señorita."

"But the black boy's father came for you with the policeman because you gave his son a bloody nose."

"Señorita, I ran away."

"He says you hit him with your satchel."

Along with my astonishment, a strange daring welled up inside me like a strong liquor spreading through my body and altering my sense of the meaning of things. I was overcome by an impulse to

grab something, with a feeling of possible mastery. I stared aimlessly at the plants and my teacher's white arms, without seeing
any precise detail; everything seemed to bulge within a thick,
soggy atmosphere. The colors of the objects fit very neatly into
their contours. I felt voracious and ready to manhandle all these
things in joyful mayhem. If necessary, I could have found it within
myself to stray from the path of virtue; I didn't know whether I
was going to be a gentleman or a pirate. It's true that no such success befell me, but henceforth I would try by every means to hit
with my own fists.

The intoxication soon passed. It was a long time before I finally
did have my go at fighting. The black boy didn't pick on me again,
though one day he caught up with me and asked for a copper coin.

I loved my teacher and was grateful to her because she'd saved
me from the police, but the moment she turned her head away I
couldn't help running my eyes over her bare arms.

After finishing my homework one night, I read a book in which
a bandit went down a road lined with *abedules*—birch trees. I
didn't know what *abedules* were but imagined they were plants. I
stopped reading because I was very sleepy, but I went to bed with
the word *abedules* on my lips. As I lay there, I thought about how
people had given names to things. I didn't know if they had
thought up the names in order to be able to remember things that
weren't there, or if they'd had to guess at names that things had already had before people learned them. It might also have been that
the people back then already had certain names in mind, and then
proceeded to distribute them among things. If that were the case, I
would have chosen *abedules* as the name for caresses given to a
white arm: the *abe* would be the full part of the white arm and the
dules would be the fingers caressing it. I turned on the light, took
my notebook and pencil from my satchel, and wrote, "I want to
give my teacher *abedules*." Then I found the eraser, erased everything, and put out the light. The next day my teacher wrinkled up

her forehead over something I'd written, and it was the phrase I'd written down the night before, and not entirely erased. As she read it, she asked, "I want to give my teacher what?" I struggled a while to get out the word *abedules*, but when she wanted to know why I'd put it there I balked and she had to give up. Then she said, "What an odd boy he is!"

One afternoon I began imagining what would happen if I were to caress one of my teacher's arms, and I came very close to doing it, but then realized it would be easier to try to start a fight with my fists than to caress my teacher with my fingertips.

The last time I saw her she was very lovely. It was at the university; I was about to take the entrance exam. She suffered a great deal, poor lady, because just before the exam she asked me, "How many grams are in a kilo?" and to my great misfortune I chose to answer with the number six. (Later she told my mother about it in a very pained letter.)

There was no need for me to take the oral exam. By chance, my name was the first one called when they were announcing those eliminated by the written exam. My father, who'd bought some neckties to give me if I passed, had to give them to me to help me get over the shame, instead. I remember the moment he gave them: I was crying, sitting on a trunk behind a curtain.

I awoke from my memories; the Mandolión was sleeping. When we arrived at a station, he let out a few more snores; it may have been the silence that woke him up. As long as he was asleep, he didn't inspire unpleasant thoughts; he slept as if he still belonged to his mother and she were saying at every moment, "Poor little fellow, look how he fell asleep!"

As soon as he woke up he started to stretch, clenching his fists, which went white. As he stretched, the life preserver grew larger and this time he noticed it and began tucking his shirt into his pants. Then we spoke of various things. It took an effort for me to follow him—his ideas lurched as if they were drunk. Just when they seemed to be heading in one direction, they'd veer off in another but would then scurry back to the same place, and I didn't know how they were going to connect. In the end I managed to gain a solid understanding of the following concepts: "Buenos Aires is bigger than Montevideo. Buenos Aires might as well be the capital of Montevideo."

At noon he bought bananas. He ate one, then wanted to open the window to throw the peel away, but he needed both hands to open the window and was holding the peel in one, so he decided to throw it on the floor instead. The window remained shut and the heel of his yellow boot pushed the banana peel out of sight under the seat.

Now I had to sit still and face the great void of the journey, warding off all the things that were trying to fill that void. As soon as I stopped concentrating on this, the Mandolión would take up residence in my eyes. But if, to get rid of the Mandolión, I turned my eyes to the window, the landscape, which had been spinning through them for so long, wearied me. And I had already meditated quite enough on the situation I'd blundered into. A few days before, when I arrived at the café where I was playing—one of Montevideo's finest—I found all the mirrors covered with big white letters announcing a new orchestra for the following day. The owner was very happy with us and had promised us three years of work, but three months later—with the season already in full swing—he hired an all-girl orchestra and we were out in the street. Our orchestra disbanded and I took this new job. It would allow me to go on paying off debts to the banks, and if I managed to take over the classes that a teacher who'd recently come to live in Montevideo had left behind down there, I could send for my wife. But this present version of what my thoughts were is far too abridged, for back then I wasn't quite sure where the train would leave us.

I'd been to that city before, when I was a boy. I vaguely remembered that I'd gone there with other boys—we all belonged to an organization—and since there wasn't much water a few of us all had to bathe in the same water, and I was among the last to have a turn before the tub was drained. I also remembered the roads, which were dirt or covered with a reddish gravel the color of wet bricks. With that same organization for boys—something like the English Boy Scouts—I had continued on to Chile, crossing the Argentine province of Mendoza and the Andes on foot. It was the period when we were studying history, and we knew when the centennial of the battle of Chacabuco, won by San Martín, would be. All the "scouts" of America had been invited to assemble for the centennial; there would be a vast gathering on the battlefield of Chacabuco. Four of us were going from Uruguay: three boys and the leader, a man who fought desperately to preserve that organization and who called it the Vanguard of the Fatherland. I was fourteen and it was the first time I'd been so far away from my family, and for such a long time: the excursion lasted a little over a month. We walked about five hundred kilometers and climbed to a height of over four thousand meters.

I now believe that at that point in my life I traveled without memories. Instead, I was creating them, and I intervened in things for the purpose of creating them, but my actions were negligible compared to those of my companions: I waited for life like someone absently eating a meal. I was always the last to understand, and quite often I only pretended to have understood. During our train ride from Buenos Aires to Mendoza I didn't create many memories; those I did create were mainly physical, such as my discomfort as I tried out different positions on the second-class seats, made of varnished planks that came up to the middle of my back; at night I didn't know where to let my head fall and it bobbled like a streetlight that has almost gone out. The memories I created during the day didn't leave any anguish in me; even when I was tired, things happened as if I were entertaining myself by playing soli-

taire or looking at illustrations in a book. I remember the shape of
the bread—more like cake, really—that women would be selling in
the stations along the way; when they started talking to each other
their voices made a little song that rose and fell across charming
mountains. That area of the Pampas was flat. We crossed another
region that was filled with a dust so fine that although we closed
the windows our eyebrows and hair went white with it. The last
memory I have of that stage of the journey is filled with vineyards
reaching to the horizon.

There are memories that live in dimly lit spaces; then they
reappear and I feel again the moments when we approached and
entered the dark belt of the night, the belt that separated the two
days of that journey.

Near the station, a little before nightfall, as the train was slow-
ing down, the sky that loomed over my window was unexpectedly
blocked out several times by some big dark tank-cars standing on
the next track. It was the first time I'd seen such monstrosities, but
I had prepared my soul not to be overly astonished by the things
men make. I didn't know how to think about what the world was
like before there were any of those tank-cars or any other huge
thing, or the effort of having made it; I didn't much believe in
things that were truly huge and fantastical. When I was a boy, if I
was told that a marvelous play was being performed in a theatre, I
always came out disillusioned, as if I'd been hoping that my fellow
men could make the roof of the theater fly off, and make things far
more wondrous than those that emerged from the wings of the
poor stage appear from the sky.

That night I felt a sudden hostility towards the tank-cars and an
impassioned sympathy for the sky. And when the train had passed
all the tank-cars and I saw the sky again, it didn't seem to belong to
the lands beneath it, but to be the sky of other places farther ahead
that I didn't yet know.

As the sky slowly went out, my eyes opted to take in the things

inside the train. The yellowish light in there not only impover-
ished everything but made it look suspicious, as well. Some bundles, all belonging to a single passenger, had gathered in one spot
and were holding each other close; their bulges, on which the dim
light shone down directly, looked like eyelids closed by sleep, but at
the same time the bundles seemed to be peering out from cracks in
the shadows, though you didn't know where the eyes' pupils were.
By day they'd been indifferent; when we didn't look at them they
slid slowly away, and all at once we found them in another spot.
Looking at them helped us remember the various places we'd
passed through, but now there were very few of us left beneath the
yellowish light and they looked at us warily. I was a little hungry
because there was canned tongue to eat that night but no bread to
go with it. Revolted after just a few bites, two of us gave our share
to the third, who ate all the tongue and the aspic, as well.

Only now do I realize that the theme of hunger began in the
train; the happy events in Mendoza and throughout much of the
journey were spoiled by hunger, and the development of this great
theme had consequences that not only raised the sky we later
found above us, but formed clouds in it that began to glide in the
direction opposite ours, passing over places we'd left behind and
changing the light on the happy memories. Not only did I appear
to be the author of a great betrayal, but my adolescent imagination
led me to believe that because of me a conflict would break out between the nations of Argentina and Uruguay.

In Mendoza, we stayed at the home of the leader of the local
"scouts." A while after our arrival, I was enjoying some solitude,
pleasantly submerged in a warm bath. The water came up to my
neck, and the bathroom's white tiles reached almost to the ceiling.
I was looking at the objects that had been left in there with me and
thinking of the people who had been in the parlor with me a
minute before. I'd played the piano and conversed with the girls
who lived in that house—who also belonged to the "scouts" and

would also cross the mountains on foot. The people in that house, always quick to shower us with their generous warmth, gazed upon us as if the great good luck of having us there with them had been brought about by some magical procedure. But they thought of us as if across the distance that separated our two countries. No doubt they wanted to draw conclusions from our behavior, to give them an idea of what Uruguayans were like. But we were very different from each other, and while they might find some things in common—our way of using or pronouncing certain words—we continually threw them off track in other respects and made them move their heads in all directions. Even I had no definite ideas about my companions; each one produced a different feeling in me, a feeling that appeared whenever I encountered their bodies, which moved around and said things in their voices, each so different, forming a rush of words within their mouths. But the oldest of the three of us took more care with his words, and had taken care to dress correctly, as well. His body was on the tall side and his back, which was only slightly curved, looked as if he were just embarking on a polite bow. With that and a smile he could stay afloat on any social surface. What was more, he seemed to have abandoned his secret land at a very young age; he had forded a river and was now on the other side with the world, exchanging smiles and dance steps. And since he was blond and fair, he seemed a higher quality article in society than the other two of us, with our black hair and olive skin. While he quickly stepped forward into the arena of courtesy—where someone else always seemed to be waiting for him, having had the same idea at the same moment—we remained firmly planted over here on this side. My second companion—the other olive-skinned boy, the one who'd eaten the tongue and its aspic without bread—existed inside his body as if within a wall that slumbered on the bank of a river. When someone called out to him from the other bank, he had to dash outside himself; he couldn't stay afloat like the blond boy, but answered very softly, stammering and looking as if he were swallowing water. When it crinkled, his skin seemed made of some very rigid material and the olive color changed to white at the crinkles. After the instant of being addressed had passed, the tension that produced his smile relaxed, but his black eyes remained among the people— where the blond boy was bending slightly forward—still watching everyone out of some elemental instinct while he would return to the other side, where I was. Behind the gaze he left on the others, his astute thoughts were working in secret, and even though his sturdy body was close to mine, toiling in its inner lands and not participating in the action, his thoughts were closer to the blond boy's and he would later talk over the other people's lives with him. That was when I gave free rein to my astonishment. They spoke of the others as if I weren't there. It's true that they were older—the one with olive skin had two years on me and the blond boy four—but the same thing happened to me with children younger than I was. I could almost say that even when we were all very small it was apparent that they were going to become grown-ups and I would remain a minor my whole life. Whenever one of them met another—especially if it was for the first time, and however much spontaneous warmth they felt for each other—he would start trying to dress the other in one of two suits, the sharp suit or the dimwit suit, with a furtiveness that seemed natural. The second fellow had only to pull on a sleeve or one leg of the pants for the first one forever after to think of and see the second in the suit he had initially brought over for him to put on. The struggle over the two suits could remain friendly for a long time; it would be waged behind the words they were speaking, and peace was often maintained by the illusion of each that he was obviously the one wearing the sharp suit and seeing the other fellow in the dimwit suit. There were also friendships in which one member acknowledged his own dimwit suit and admired the other guy's sharp suit. The position I found myself in was more unusual: hardly had someone new entered the room then I'd already raised an arm or a leg to begin donning the dimwit suit. At first the other fellow would be disconcerted by the ease with which this happened—was this guy slipping a dimwit suit on over a sharp suit? But it didn't take long to ascertain that I had only one suit, and when he found out that I played the piano, he would think, "Of course: he's thinking about music. They probably had him study piano because he's a dimwit." In the best of cases, they would see me as a useful tool for times when they had to sing the national anthem or needed to dance, or to include "a classical piece" among a gathering's various entertainments.

That afternoon at the scout leader's house in Mendoza, a moment came when it seemed appropriate for me to play "a classical piece." That was what they called pieces that couldn't be danced to, and along with Beethoven's "Pathétique" Sonata, people of little culture placed under that heading a song called "The Widow's Tears" and a nocturne of my own recent composition. The first piece I played that afternoon was Schubert's "Serenade," in an arrangement that fragmented it, though its different parts, thrown carelessly down among weeds and artificial flowers, were still recognizable. There were some arpeggios at the beginning of the piece, as if the muse were preparing her harp. I believe the arpeggios ran from high to low, which always makes listeners think of a waterfall. In another part, the melody took the form of repeated, scintillating octaves, and at that point many people sighed without realizing it.

Then I played my nocturne. It opened with a series of great, grave chords; I played them with my hands spread wide, at the deliberate pace of a medium placing her hands on the table and awaiting the arrival of the spirits. Those chords aroused an expectant silence, casting heavy, sonorous storm clouds over the atmosphere. I felt like an artist who presses down hard on the pencil and puts in a lot of black.

They applauded and praised me. But suddenly everyone paused. A young lady had risen to her feet, filled her lungs with air, raised her shoulders, opened her mouth and nostrils wide, and turned her eyes towards some distant point; at first I wasn't quite sure whether or not she was going to recite something, and her stance sent my thoughts wavering between the infinite and a sneeze.

The big, black grand piano, like a somnolent old animal crouched on its thick paws, meekly endured the hands that slammed down on its yellow teeth and filled its innards with loud noises. A few of us took turns at that. Finally, I asked for a short melody, three or four notes long, to improvise upon. I was prepared for this the way a lady is prepared for the photographer to take her by surprise. I would insert the melody they gave me into forms or structures I'd tried out many times before, for I had long practice at the game of improvisation; I'd first heard it done by Clemente Colling—a French organist—and had then copied the procedure. (I imitated him the way a child of two imitates someone writing or reading the newspaper.) At first, no one could ever understand what I proposed to do: they'd tell me they didn't know how to give melody or things like that; then I'd tell them that even without knowing anything about music they could press three different keys, one after the other, like taking three rolls out of a bag. At last someone who knew music would decide to do it, almost always giving me the three notes of a common arpeggio, and that was very easy, but if the notes were provided by someone who didn't know music the tune would lend itself to something stranger, the listeners might pay more attention to its development, and the experiment would have more interesting results. People who had never before realized that a melody is a repeating pattern found that to be of interest; they enjoyed recognizing the melody in a variety of presentations, as it was altered and imbued with different hues by changes of tonality and exposed to all sorts of hazards over the course of the improvisation. Though the ignorance I was constructing that course out of was quite innocent, I sometimes suspected that my audacity would strike anyone capable of understanding the techniques I was employing as disrespectful. I had certain forms in mind, but the tune would sometimes force me to seek out other, new ones; then I grabbed hold of any sonorous filler at hand; and the more trouble I thought I was in, the more I raised the tide of sound, for if the music was loud enough the notes of the melody only needed to float across it like the unsubmerged corners of familiar household objects. Then the tide fell and I would play slow chords while the listeners waited for something and I did, too; the slow chords gave me time to think. The silences between them impressed people as either ridiculous or historic; some of them thought of the biographies of musicians they'd read in the newspapers, and under the sway of that prestige their imaginations turned toward the specimen they had in front of them.

My companions would say, "Well, no wonder he's a dimwit!" And they would feel proud, flaunting the fact that they'd been in on a plan no one else had anticipated; our organization's representatives had had the foresight to come equipped with a pianist. My companions may even have said that "back home" there were lots of pianists and improvisers like "this guy." Of course they wouldn't say I was a dimwit; on the contrary, they would hide it and try to explain that I was distracted and had my eccentricities, as mystics do. But deep within themselves they believed that nothing could compensate for the disgrace of being a dimwit: being sharp was the first principle of mankind, more important than health; sharpness meant you'd always be able to get whatever you needed and was an even greater source of pride than bravery. To be sharp was the crucial fighting instinct and the glory of the intellect. However, they were to discover certain widespread injustices in the appreciation of this principle, especially among girls. I didn't know how to approach girls the way the blond boy did, nor did I hurl my being outside myself when called, like the other olive-skinned boy. I went among girls as if I'd gone strolling through a forest and suddenly found that I'd emerged from the forest and entered a city, whose din was forcing me to notice it. Perhaps the people I'd entrusted my footsteps to had led me there. I never asked anyone to explain why I'd been taken there, but resigned myself as if to the inexplicable transitions of a dream. What was more, I would never entirely feel that I was in the city; I would carry around a bit of forest like a deep inner conviction, making the same movements I'd been making among the trees, and at certain moments the girls became joyous plants in a forest clearing. I was long accustomed to these surprises and from my own place I would signal to them as if I were another plant. And suddenly, inventing a puff of air to move them and bring them near, they would brush me with their leaves. At those times I watched their movements without breathing, but with an attentive heart. I wouldn't hear all the words they said because one of their words would suddenly fall into a place from which a path instantly emerged, leading away from the clearing. But before long it led back. I would find them angry; they'd discovered that I was a dimwit, and would tell me off, and then I would make my way into the heart of the forest, thinking of them. And then the strangest thing of all would happen: still believing I was a dimwit, they would, even so, look at me as if looking at a tangled forest; they would see beyond the dimwit. At the same time their gazes would be lost, and they would gaze in the opposite direction, as if at a place behind their own eyes, a secret past, for they, too, had a forest, and it hadn't been very long since they'd abandoned it. Then one of them would come back, to brush me with her leaves.

There was one girl who was very fat and had hair as short as ours. I didn't like her—though I acknowledged one charming thing about her: the two large gold rings hooked through her ears, which were evocations of a woman on the head of a boy—but that fat girl seemed to be the other olive-skinned boy's ideal. He spoke to her with the smile that made his cheeks crinkle and go pale, which the cheeks avenged by invading his eyes and making them small. She attended to him with a few words, then turned her head to tell me something she knew about some musicians. I gathered up my strength and addressed myself to the girl I did like: the one who seemed poised between the infinite and a sneeze before she recited. It would have been indiscreet to run my eyes over the whole height and girth of her body. She had squeezed it into a dress that was white with black lines running across it like meridians. The only skin visible was on her face and around her blue eyes, and it was very white. Above it she had a golden crown that sprang from her own head: she wore her braids in a coil around her head. She was twice my age. I gazed upon her as upon a goddess, and from very far below: she spoke only a few words to me, some of which were to ask me to sit down, for she was about to recite. When she stood up, a great distance opened between us.

When the afternoon was over and it was my turn to have a bath, and I was left alone in the bathroom, the momentum generated by the people in the parlor lasted a good while longer. It took an effort to relocate myself, for I was still gripped by the excitement of answering all the questions and embarking upon all the velocities of all the people who'd approached me. There in the bathroom I continued on, almost as if I were still surrounded by people. I was someone else, watching myself as I ran the bath and took my clothes off, but all of that was slow compared to the momentum I'd brought in from the parlor. Then I started whistling. As soon as I felt air on my pursed lips I realized that I was the one who was whistling and that it was false, that I didn't feel like whistling and was having a hard time being alone. Finally, fatigue and the disappointment or distance that had arisen between me and the poetry reciter began to depress me. But in a little while I was calm again in the warm water. As I slowly revolved a bar of greenish soap whose fragrance was new to me in my half-open hand, and after I'd floated for a while in the warm water with my memories and spread the slick soap across my arms, I felt something: an uncharacteristic will to inquire into certain things.

I'd never been much at ease with my body or even had much knowledge of it. I maintained certain clear or obscure relations with it, but always with intermittences in the form of lengthy oblivions or sudden bursts of attention. The members of my family were better acquainted with my body. At home, they'd raised it like a small animal; they were fond of it and treated it solicitously. When I set off on this journey, they commended it to my care. At first I traveled with it as if it were an innocent creature that I was annoyed at having become responsible for. But I soon grew distracted and was happy. At home I could be distracted for long periods of time; they took care of my body and I could attend to what passed before my eyes: my eyes were like a small, portable screen that capriciously registered anything the world projected. And I could also give myself over to whatever came into my head—the eyes' memories or inventions. I could do that even while walking, because at home if I went off the wrong way they stood in front of me with their arms opened wide and my body turned and moved in another direction. Away from home, my body was perfectly capable of hurling itself into an abyss, and me with it. I've always felt it living beneath my thoughts. Sometimes my thoughts gather in some part of my head to deliberate behind closed doors; they forget the body. Sometimes the body is prudent and doesn't interrupt them, only sending news of its existence when it's tired or sad or some part of it hurts. I don't know who brings that news or what paths it takes to the head. The new arrival knocks softly, pushes open the door to the gathered thoughts, and is immediately transformed into another thought; coming to an understanding with the rest, that thought delivers the news: far away, on a foot, a toenail is ingrown. At first the other thoughts pay no heed to the newcomer, telling him to wait a moment and even getting mad at him, but the newcomer insists and the others are forced grudgingly to suspend their meeting and do something else; they must become other thoughts and concern themselves with the body. The body, in turn, has to disturb all its regions, and the whole body stands up, limps off to heat up some water, pours it into a basin and finally places the ingrown toenail in it. Then the thoughts go back to being other thoughts, the ones gathered behind closed doors, and they forget the body and the toenail still soaking in the basin.

I believe that thoughts inhabit the whole body, though not all of them travel to the head to be clothed in words. I know that some thoughts walk barefoot through the body. When the eyes seem to be absent—their gaze lost because the intellect has withdrawn for a few moments and left them empty while the thoughts in the head deliberate behind closed doors—the barefoot thoughts move up through the body and settle in the eyes. From there, like snakes that hypnotize birds, they seek an object to fix the gaze on. They also hypnotize the thoughts in the closed meeting, forcing them to abandon their deliberations.

That afternoon—when I had just been shown the bathroom and the door to the hallway was still open—I smiled in the enchantment of being offered a place and some objects that belonged to the intimate life of people I had only recently met. I could hardly explain this privilege to myself; I accepted it as children accept something the grown-ups have prepared for them. But after closing the door and whistling as I tried out this new way of being alone, I felt those barefoot thoughts beginning to rise through my body. Perhaps the objects left in there with me had provoked them. What was more, the objects had something of their owners' smiling benevolence, and I couldn't help thinking that they were offering themselves to me—I'm referring to other objects besides those authorized to approach me and which I could pick up with no qualms, in the certainty that they had to participate in the act of the bath. And although these objects were innocuous, I'd had occasion in the past to grow suspicious of certain types of innocence. Once before, I'd been made to wonder whether things were indeed innocuous or had some element of craftiness. Worse, I had thought about how natural it is for even a great innocence to coexist with other things that were terrible.

Shortly before stepping into the bath I discovered that my eyes were staring at a basket of dirty laundry, and barefoot thoughts were starting to make their way up through my body. It was summertime and the body was in no hurry to sink into the warm water. Then I took a few steps that brought me over to the basket where clothes unfamiliar to me lay: the body took its carnal steps over cool tiles painted with green flowers. Before the hands raised the lid of the basket, I turned my head to look towards the door, which was closed, mute, its glass panes whitish and opaque like cataracts in a blind man's eyes. In the head's round trip to the door and back, the eyes glimpsed the sparkling facets of the white tiles on the wall. Hardly had my hands started lifting the lid of the basket when I heard the "ahem" of the straw hinges, like a warning, but my eyes were already beginning to see, among other things that were white, a bit of fabric that was sky-blue, though the panel of wrinkled lace that passed under the armpits was tinted with other colors which sweat had picked up from other clothes on the same body. Pincers formed by index fingers and thumbs grasped the sky-blue cloth, extracting it in a series of little tugs, the way a magician withdraws a string of formerly separate objects, now all tied together, from a top hat. It was an undergarment, and a rather large one. I first thought of the poetry reciter but immediately recalled that she didn't live in that house, and then I remembered the other olive-skinned boy's fat girl. I dropped the garment and closed the basket. Then I had to open it again to stuff in a bit of sky blue that was sticking out. And finally it occurred to me to arrange it and cover it up exactly as I'd found it. Even so, the idea that I might have been seen continued to trouble me. What would they think if they saw a naked male with a female undergarment in his hands? Would they think I wanted to try it on? But when I forced my attention to remain on this fact—I repeated the idea to myself several times—I thought of certain meanings such an occurrence might have. An encounter had taken place between two very distinct things: my nakedness and her garment. However little soul an object may have in its own right—or may receive from its users—would still be enough to make its violation a strange occurrence. What would happen if, facing this sky-blue fabric's owner, I were to transmit this thought to her: "I was naked with a piece of your lingerie in my hands"? Perhaps, if the person I encountered in that situation were the poetry reciter, a thought of hers would have answered mine: "You idiot, what does it matter that you had my underwear in your hands if I wasn't wearing it at the time?"

It was then that I felt a certain depression. My body and I were disappointed. It had dragged me along on a dismal adventure, and in addition to being sad we were both conscious of having committed a betrayal. The bathroom had been loaned to us simply so that we could bathe, or rather, it had been loaned to me so I could bathe my body. But my body generally forgot everything and took responsibility for nothing. It surrendered to the warm water as if allowing itself to be pampered by a sweetheart. The water kept the flesh afloat, allowing the arms and legs to move freely, but in fact, as it rose around the chest, the water was a little oppressive; the body had to quicken its breathing, overcome by a certain forced cheerfulness. Finally, the tickling surface of the water reached the neck.

Although I saw my body contentedly playing with the water, I was sad. Then, as my body sniffed the soap and the water rippled almost imperceptibly, I turned my gaze, like an immobile shadow—and certain thoughts were floating in that shadow—onto the water.

I was disappointed, not only by the scant attention the poetry reciter had paid to me and the dismal adventure my body had taken me on, but also by what had happened between my body and me as a result of the performance of a piece of music.

At no time could I dismount from my body. And this forced co-existence exposed me to all sorts of risks. I certainly didn't want to be rid of it or even to neglect it (if it died on me I didn't have the slightest hope of surviving, and when it got sick it was far too demanding), and my body was also what furnished me with the comforts I needed in order to penetrate the mysteries to which my imagination was drawn. (I suspect that this passion came to me largely from my body, as did all the violences I needed to abandon myself to when not in a state of contemplation.) After my body and I had committed an act of violence—such as unleashing ourselves on the piano—we were left with a feeling of emptiness. And in this the body had a very important role. No sooner did it see a piano than it became like a locomotive starting to build up steam. If any girls were present, it didn't move, but threw more coal into the furnace. If the girls played first, it seemed on the verge of exploding; when those present asked it if I would play, I could no longer control it, not even to make it politely wait until I'd been asked a few times; already envisioning the storm clouds of the nocturne emerging from its head, it was off. It saw itself take a few steps and sit down at the piano. Just as I would improvise a piece of music, the body—knowing it was being watched—would improvise movements. I was watching it, too, as if I were observing another person whose movements I was trying to correct, for they were as slow as the motion of a tiger drawing near its prey. The moment would come to astonish everyone with its pounce, but in the meantime the attention of the spectators had to be held and the promise of great things had to be suggested. It felt the stares on its flanks and bristled with emotion. At first, it modulated the chords and phrasing of a simple melody with slow passion. But it couldn't linger for long in vales of sighs; the attention of those who understand very little demands variety. Then the pounces began. And there, too, began the disaster. The excitement of the pounces grew too quickly and the desire to astonish was also impatient, exaggerating the tempo and soon beginning to lose control; then it resorted, all too quickly, to every tactic, and the tactics, passing through the imagination at top speed, couldn't manage to be implemented; the wild beast, in pursuit of the escaping prey, was destroying everything in its path. But the path was no longer a path—a rushing current was carrying me and my body away; we flailed out ridiculously, hopelessly, trying to find something to grasp on the banks, which were receding, and we concluded our execution of the piece in a state of unconsciousness. The spectators applauded madly; the anguish I so sincerely felt over this disaster was, to them, the artistic expression of an uncontrollable passion. In addition to leaving me and my body empty and disappointed, this caused a distance to arise between it and me. After the applause I left the piano and walked towards the front hall; I was extremely upset. I was ashamed that I'd been in the clearing where the girls were, and that I'd thought about them; I was trying to enter my forest and be alone to nurse my shame, but I couldn't quite get away: I circled around the clearing where they were commenting on my "success" and watched them, hiding among low trees and concealing my face behind broad leaves. But then the girls came to find me and persuade me to play again, and I curtly refused. It was all very sad; they were praising me for virtues I knew very well I did not possess. The one thing I had and they didn't was my sadness at playing badly only to witness so false a success and see it applauded by these serious people who lived in such touching ignorance.

The body was dismayed by the fact that I'd allowed the girls to plead with me for so long—or what seemed to it like so long—to go back and play again, letting them keep their eyes fixed on me for all that time and make so many movements with their lips over teeth that were so white, and then hadn't granted any request, but watched them turn and walk away, with their heads, their waists, and their legs.

My body, continually being notified of that reality, was trying to make me understand that I had to be like the girls, who remained so fresh after issuing forth the monotonous current of their performances; the written music seemed to pass through the external part of their eyes into the nose, then the hands, until it finally reached the piano, sweeping leaves and bits of wood and paper along in its wake, detritus that did no more than change position in the noisy monotony of that current.

Then the gathering broke up, before I'd managed to yield to the temptation of playing once more. And in the bathtub that afternoon, I thought that I should give up the piano. I remembered how long I'd been studying the piece that had just come out so badly, and I knew none of my fellow students would have had to work as hard: they had clearer heads—their wits were less dim—and better memories. Even the girls who were so mediocre played more fluidly than I did. And to think that when I first heard one of the pieces that made me crazy with pleasure I would swear to study it for nights, days, years, whatever it took to learn it. Some pieces had an impassioned anguish to them, an anguish attained only in certain passages, yet as you listened to the piece a second time you waited for those passages and the anguish extended across the entire work; I would sense that sad substance in a turn or involuntary movement of the waist of a body of white sounds, and though the movement was slow, not all the senses could comprehend it and there was no full awareness of its pleasure: these waves revealed parts of a body without fulfilling the desire to see all of it. But the part that could be perceived was sweetly sorrowful, and although it seemed new, you discovered that it had been waiting to be awoken, hiding, full of warmth, in a secretly favored place in your past. And while you were listening to it, your eyes repeatedly glanced at various parts of a single object; it could be a glass vase, whose burgundy color extended to mingle with other objects. At times, without recalling the notes of a melody, I could remember the feeling it had given me and what I'd been looking at when I heard it. One evening as I was listening to a brilliant piece while staring out the window, my heart came out of my eyes and absorbed a house many stories tall that I saw across the way. Another night, in the penumbra of a concert hall, I heard a melody floating upon ocean waves that a great orchestra was making; in front of me, on a fat man's bald pate, gleamed a little patch of light; I was irritated and wanted to look away, but since the only comfortable position for my eyes left my gaze resting on the gleam of that pate, I had no choice but to allow it to enter my memory along with the melody, and then what always happens happened: I forgot the notes of the melody— displaced by the gleaming pate—and the pleasure of that moment remains supported in my memory only by the bald pate. Then I decided always to look at the floor whenever I was listening to music. But once, when a lady behind me was with a very young child, I saw water appear between my own feet, gliding along like a viper, and then suddenly its head began to grow larger in a depression in the floor and eyes of foam came running along the liquid body to gather in the head.

When I was at a gathering or a concert, listening to a piece that enthused me—I was always ready to feel enthusiasm for any piece—and I decided to learn it, I clutched that idea tightly with my whole soul because I knew it might escape me, or rather I should say that I knew I would abandon it if I heard another piece I liked better within the next few days. So at that moment I clung to the piece before me, not in the aim of being faithful to the work

that was making me so happy, but because, knowing I might be un-
faithful to it, I had a stubborn urge to keep this immediate possibility of pleasure from escaping me. Furthermore, I thought I
should take advantage of the time that remained before I became
enthused with another piece by mastering this first one: in that
way neither one would escape me. I felt an anguished greed to have
them all between my fingers, to carry them always with me, and I
imagined in advance the muscular pleasures of holding their
sonorous bodies in my hands and mastering their movements. Just
how I would play and hold this or that piece, making its melodious
voice suffer, depended on the nature of my urge.

It was very important not to tell anyone that I liked a piece; the
moment I allowed my passion to show I would be obliged to
demonstrate what my conduct would be towards this piece I liked
so much, and how I would later come to play it. Not only did the
adventure then lose part of its charm, it also ceased to be an adventure that was mine alone, and other people were given a part in it.
But if I remembered, as I plunged into the street with the secret
purpose of seeing what would happen to me when I found the
piece and learned it, that other people had heard the piece at the
concert and it had belonged to all of them a little bit, I thought
they must have forgotten it by now: the piece would be mine alone.
Then I quickened my steps until my legs ached; I was going to
meet it without knowing where I would find it, as if I were going in
search of a woman who was sleeping somewhere in a forest, and
though she didn't know me, it would be my privilege to pick her
up and initiate all sorts of affinities with her. Though many others
had played her and she had known them all, she would have no
choice now but to allow me a personal experience, and in that experience she would be completely different and completely mine.
And though the piece had already been heard by many people, if
no one else in Montevideo had thought of studying it—I'm referring to a piece introduced to us by a touring concert pianist—then

I would have the privilege of taking her home with me and locking myself in with her as if I were detaining a foreign lady. Though there were several copies at the music center, I still thought that she was a single, lone thing; seeing several copies was like having double vision. Giving the clerk no time to wrap her up for me, I came out with the piece in my hands. On the way back to my piano I tripped over a thousand things as I looked at and away from the piece a thousand times, and before I got there I already knew the smell of her paper and ink by heart.

Finally, when I'd closed myself in with her in the parlor of my house, I placed her on the music stand like a man placing an image upon an altar. My hands, as clumsily as someone groping for something with his head turned in another direction—or as if he had a handkerchief over his eyes—began the ceremony immediately. I was hoping that the sounds I'd heard at the concert would come: perhaps my hands could summon them as the concert pianist's hands had at the moment when all of us realized, in silence, that the sounds rising from his fingers were becoming an impassioned presence: she was revealing herself, reclining across a slow scattering of time as if on a bed she herself had prepared for eternity. Now it was my turn to discover the circumstances under which these sounds would unite their secret proximities, and then the miracle would appear.

My happiest surprise came from the coincidence that the melody, which easily revealed the work I wanted to recognize, was also the easiest part to play.

In the places where slow melodies were written, there was more white space on the paper; the notes were scattered around capriciously—in the center of the staff, along its edges, or beyond them—but almost always in open spaces and at considerable distance from each other. Suddenly, arriving at a place where there was a chord, I would pause, as if in the shade of a strange tree in a new country; then I would go back to following the trail of the notes, so whimsically strewn about. When I recognized the melody from the concert—now come back to live in the hollow of my hands as they labored, face down—I would repeat it a thousand times until I'd left it exhausted and senseless. Only then would I begin concerning myself with the work's outlying regions, and attempt to penetrate the labyrinths where the paper was black with a dense undergrowth of signs. First I ran my eyes across that forest as if flying over it in an airplane, trying to spot each area's particular flora, and then I began the slow hike across it on foot. However cautious I was, I always took some false steps; after stumbling, I would start over again, thinking I could find another way in and trying somehow to wade through the difficult passages. At such moments I worked in silence and hoped to encounter something that would surprise me, but since I had to be continually alert to their position on the map I could barely comprehend what the sounds were meant to be. I couldn't decipher the noises in that forest until some time had gone by and I was more familiar with its life. But desperate at having to stay in one place for too long, I made useless efforts, going through the same motions many times in blind determination. I made fanciful contortions and my hands, reduced to a state of tense immobility, became small knots of hobbled effort; my impassioned quest to move ahead trapped me in that tension which, bit by bit, gripped fingers, hands, wrists, shoulders, and legs until my whole body was stiff. Only then did I rest, but as I rested I imagined what it would be like to play the piece in front of girls. I was very shy; while I was seated at a piano, the girls would approach the edges of the keyboard, and I would shoot fleeting glances at them which I would rapidly reel back in, since I had to pay attention to what I was playing.

What pained me was that the most difficult passages were generally the least interesting ones; any transition—any simple anxiety with which the composer had sullied the depths of the time gliding by—required an effort far greater than its importance warranted, but I had to learn the whole piece; this was the tribute I had to pay if I wanted to be seen with her or stroll about with her in public. I calculated how much I could learn in a single day and therefore how long it would take to reach the end. But all my calculations were false: it either took much more time or else I got fed up with the piece long before I was through. After some time had gone by, and I'd had other illusions and failures with other pieces, one day, by chance, I'd go back to that one. And after many fits and starts, I would at last succeed in playing it all the way through.

That afternoon in Mendoza I'd performed a piece for the first time, thinking that although I hadn't yet entirely mastered it, I might, by great effort, have an extraordinary adventure: I imagined moments of a passion heretofore unknown to me, for not only did I not know what impression the piece would make on its listeners, I didn't know what it might do to me, either. Furthermore, I needed to show off, and I was curious to see what the others would say. When the disaster occurred, I was furious with my body, but afterwards I could only imagine that a kind of strange understanding existed between my body and me. The moment I began playing in front of other people, my body was suddenly unafraid; on the contrary, it swelled with pretensions that would have been very difficult to fulfill, summoning up every dream I'd ever had to demand that it pour all the future it had dreamed of into the present moment. The body looked down at its ten fingers as if from the height of an orchestra conductor who has at his feet the pit beyond the edge of the stage, where ten miserable musicians struggle madly to serve him. His head, held high in the pride of his dreams, imagined that at the end of this segment of the program he would move upstage and his hands would be clasped by the hands of pale women who would lead him to the center; he would bow before the deafening audience, and, lowering his eyelids, he wouldn't cast a single glance at the ten musicians down in the pit. But that afternoon in Mendoza, things took a different course. At first the body expected its dreams to reach an immediate understanding with the sounds. But then those ten wretches down in the pit began betraying it. Even so, it was all really the conductor's fault; on the one hand, the pride of his dreams had led him to put a distance between himself and the fellows down in the pit, a distance riddled with lapses of memory, like a bridge full of holes, and on the other hand he had tyrannized those poor wretches with his blind passion, stripping them of the freedom they would have needed in order to serve him better. And what was more, if his passion hadn't blinded him from the beginning, he would have shown some concern for each one's life and interests when he was working and practicing along with them, and they would have responded to him better. But now his pride and passion were being severely chastised. When he saw that they couldn't do what he was ordering them to do, then and only then did he seek to demonstrate some concern for each individual, as a last, desperate measure. When they began going stiff—each one's muscles knotting up and muddling the game they were supposed to be playing with their companions—everything was thrown off balance, and they started to hug each other like the vulgar members of a team. And it was then that the director began lowering his proud head little by little and leaning his body forward as if going into a crouch; he was trying to communicate with each one separately, but they'd all merged into a single shapeless mass that was holding up the game, and those moments of standstill were becoming apparent in anguished silences that did not correspond to the work. Then, when the conductor tried to move them again, the whole mass would shift, but he couldn't manage to separate them from each other. Finally, he himself plunged into the snarl of limbs and the thing ended he knew not how, all of them sprawled together in the pit.

I was remembering all that on the journey I was now taking in the company of the Mandolión. I'm sure that in the nine years that had elapsed between the two journeys those memories of Mendoza had never had as full and spacious an existence as they did now. On this second trip, all the people, things, and anguishes of the first came back to life, as if the memories had been reincarnated, as if I'd had the power to make the world revolve vertiginously backward until I found myself in the days of my adolescence again. But I didn't always manage to make the world stop at the moment I wanted; after its dizzying spin, it would oscillate and suddenly move a few days forward; at other times it went too slowly, as if snagged on some important event, or as if time were made of rubber and the world were having some difficulty stretching it. During the days we were crossing the mountains it also went slowly; perhaps it was hard to make mountains like that spin; it slowly tipped them over at night and then raised them upright again the next day with the silent patience of an old man.

At one point, as I was remembering what happened in Mendoza, the tumult of my memories industriously recomposing the past began making me anxious; my consciousness couldn't perceive all the details that were invading me in a rush; memories I had no reason to remember—for they belonged to other people's feelings and interests—kept arising, and I couldn't comprehend why certain elements of my memories had been suppressed and other things that didn't happen at that time appeared. At that moment the world spun forward a few days and, drawn by some unknown force, stopped at a simple, contemplative memory: a young woman, eating grapes beneath an arbor. When I met her there wasn't much light, but I did manage to see her eyes, covered by her eyelids; then, when she slowly opened them, it was as if she were peeling two large grapes. I'd had the pleasurable thought that she was in great need of happiness and was on the brink of silently abandoning the grapes and all the sorrows of her home to go off with me. Then I felt tired, and looked for places where I could linger a while; my eyes wanted to rest on the mountains.

Only a few moments later this memory was interrupted; I was

assailed by a strong determination to continue with the memories of Mendoza. But I not only had to turn the world back, with the weight of all its mountains, I was also sometimes interrupted by the Mandolión, and those interruptions, however insignificant, forced me to think about them and devote some slight, momentary irritation to them.

But I'm sure that despite the Mandolión I remembered a few more things about Mendoza. They happened on the night that was joined to the afternoon when I played the piano so badly and then later, in a bathroom, opened a laundry hamper.

That night, a number of boys assembled in the yard of the Mendoza scout leader's house; all of us were sitting around a very wide table, and a bright light shone from a wall onto the white tablecloth, where the gleam of glasses was distributed at intervals, along with the dark color of wine bottles standing upright and heaping platters of empanadas that looked like immobile tortoises. It's possible that there was a silence before the assault on the table began. But afterwards there was a great deal of hubbub, and the more wine we drank the more general the hubbub became. I'd drunk one glass and was already feeling tipsy. I'd been watching our leader speak with the leader from Mendoza; our leader was one of the most beloved figures of our adolescence. Regardless of whether he looked stern or a smile filled his face, he was constantly rubbing his hands hard together as if soaping them up without water. From time to time he rocked his body—which was on the small side—forward and then backwards and as he went back he lifted his toes off the ground. There was nothing to interrupt the oval line of his face, for there was no hair on the upper part of it, only some carefully blackened tufts at the sides of the temples. But within the oval, the moustache and eyebrows were very clearly marked in black. The moustache curled upwards on both sides like two sunlit peaks, and the tips rose all the way to the middle of the cheeks, which swelled when he smiled. The brows accompanied the golden arches of the glasses—two more ovals, but small and horizontal—a good bit of the way. Behind the sparkle of the glass was the sparkle of his eyes, and both the lenses and his smile made them look smaller. At that moment all the parts of his face were happily united, and the glasses, which looked like the face's adopted children, were every bit as beloved as the moustache and the eyebrows, particularly since they'd helped the eyes see better since his childhood. I was watching these small beings as if seeking to understand them all over again, and hoping that they would give me an idea that would contain all I'd ever learned about that man and could be fitted into a single word. As they gave themselves over to the play of conversation, the cheeks, which were very busy, began forming a smile; they didn't wait to find out whether the words thrown toward them by the other man's mouth were funny or not. I had my eyes wide open, because I wanted to be quick to parry the slightest suspicious expression that might escape from the other man's face. The boys had formed small groups around the table and at every moment hands and arms could be seen making incursions on the white of the tablecloth. I felt hidden by the noise; every boy's attention was completely taken up with his group's conversation, and while I appeared to be part of the group around the two conversing leaders, in fact I was paying attention only to the play of our leader's face. That was the first night I remember feeling something that only happens when many people are talking, alcohol is being drunk, the murmur of conversation is even and ongoing, and, most importantly, night lies over everything—those moments when everyone is a little tipsy from alcohol, bright light, smoke, and hubbub, and from the things moving through each of our heads, which are almost oblivious to the fact that beyond them in the darkness our destinies seem to be growing more pliable and venturing a little beyond their accustomed limits and intermingling with each other. And it's possible that the little we human beings know about one another may be best understood at such moments, even if it is all jumbled up. The paths along which each of our destinies has been growing weary, the paths along which all have come and by which all will leave, suddenly converge, and everyone stops for a rest.

As our leader was rubbing his hands together, I went on hoping that something would happen in his face and make a new idea appear to me: the idea of him that I hoped to have—that my emotions, above all, hoped for. Since that night began, I'd been in the mood for suspicions: it was a night for harboring suspicions and discovering destinies. But my head wasn't helping me. At first it had entertained itself by going about understanding the scattered things that the eyes were looking at; my head let its eyes look at anything, like a distracted mother who lets her twins run wild. Then the twins had stopped to see what would happen in the face opposite—which turned out to be the face of our leader—and that was when my emotions, which had settled comfortably behind the eyes with all the craving for suspicion that the night had provoked, started wanting to know what destiny was at work in that face, and peering out from it. Though his face was very well known to me, that night I saw it as something unfamiliar. This had also happened to me at other times with other people: it might be the light, the place they were standing, or some modification they'd made to the grooming of their face, but suddenly they had a different expression; they were like portraits of themselves that didn't entirely succeed in capturing them; and what was more they bore resemblances to other people we had never thought of comparing them with. The instability of the resemblance collided with our affection and made it waver for a moment. These people, in their resemblance to others, filled us with the anguished supposition that they might hardly recognize us or might have different and unforeseeable feelings for us; perhaps we'd been mistaken in what we had always believed ourselves to have understood. But in the face before me now things hadn't reached that point: the hands were nearby and they were a constant, never ceasing to scrub at each other vigorously. And soon there was nothing for it but to acknowledge the joyful unity of all parts of the face. If someone suddenly called out to him, he would turn his body around with a blind movement and walk over, extinguishing his smile as he went, and as you watched him move away you would think about his loyalty. But one thing was never entirely extinguished within him: a certain anxiousness. It may have sprung from his temperament, his sense of honor or that destiny of his that I wanted to know about. This anxiousness smoldered in a way that illuminated all his innocence. But he wanted to use it to protect his innocence from everything. He was a good man who always thought about bad things: he used his intelligence to foresee them. Perhaps he rubbed his hands together as a way of remaining on the alert or of being able to pick up speed very rapidly—as if he were leaving a motor running.

In addition to being our leader, he was a dentist. A few days before embarking on the great journey, he had extracted a molar from me. When I first sat down in the chair, he spoke of anything at all; he liked to talk in questions and answers: "How is it? Hmm . . . a little difficult. The molar is badly cracked. So, let's see." He went over to a glass display case, picking up and turning over objects that were unknown to me. Most of them were nickel-plated; many forms of aggression were sarcastically anticipated in them, and their gleaming restlessness was like an expectant smile a moment before leaping into action. As he picked them up and put them down—as if squeezing a loaf of bread to see if it was fresh—they alarmed or calmed me. Suddenly he picked one up for the second time; I no longer had any means of escape, but then that same instrument was abandoned for the second time. As it fell onto the glass of the tray from which he had taken it, each instrument had a different click, but all of the sounds were sharp, reminding you of enraged cries emitted by wild animals whose desire to participate had been frustrated. Perhaps their fury was building as they lay there, and if he picked them up again they would be more enraged than ever. Our leader—our dentist—seemed unsure whether he was holding the object he was seeking. Suddenly he stuck his hand into his pocket—as if the instrument might be there—took out a box of matches, and lit the alcohol lamp. There had been no talk for a while, and in the silence I was swallowing saliva at every moment, as if throwing buckets of water down to put out my burning heart. Then he came towards me, had me open my mouth, pushed his glasses up onto his forehead, squinted, and looked down as if trying to locate the ruins of a village from an airplane. He rubbed his hands a little, went over to a small table, took out a pair of tweezers, stuck their tips into a box, then pulled like someone picking up hay with a pitchfork and drew out a large wad of cotton. When he turned to come back to me, the dim light coming in through the window made his glasses flash like the headlights of a vehicle making a U-turn; when he approached me the light was behind him, obscuring his face, and the vehicle grew larger as it advanced. His short fingers, as they pushed back my lips, were like tweezers themselves; then the real tweezers put their load of cotton between lips and teeth; my mouth now had enormously thick lips and I felt something like the swelling left by a punch in the face. He returned to the little table, turned his back on me entirely, and began talking about the great journey we were going to go on to Chile. He was having a hard time getting the words out: some emerged in isolation and then a few came out all at once, like small, indecisive animals suddenly bunching together. He came towards me with a much smaller bit of cotton and rubbed my gums, and I breathed in a strong smell of alcohol. On another quick round trip he brought the shot and stabbed it very delicately into various places in my gums. He put down the syringe and, rubbing his hands together, came over to have a look at the ruins of the village. Things were filtering out from between the roots of the cracked molar and I began tasting a bitter liquid in my mouth. He was aware of this and told me to spit. As I did so, I went to join my lips together but one was missing: the upper one, immobilized by the cotton. Then I spat by pressing my lower lip against my upper teeth, like a schoolteacher showing how the labiodental "v" is pronounced. When I'd finished, he was already waiting for me, forceps in hand: its teeth were like duck's feet. He carefully placed the forceps in my mouth and the duck's feet gripped the crown of the molar: then he moved his arm like someone twisting a wet rag, but since the crown was broken the forceps slipped off; after repeating this operation several times he decided to use a different forceps. By then I was afraid, perhaps because I had felt no pain. I'd adjusted to the situation like someone who is exercising violently and hasn't yet grown tired. When he brought the other forceps, his face was odd; I thought I perceived the worried expression of a child sent out to wring a hen's neck for the first time. This latest forceps had claws like a crab, and did not lose its grip on the crown, but no matter how much force he exerted the molar did not come loose. After a while he took his glasses off and wiped away the sweat with a handkerchief in colors of half mourning. Then, with the sense of honor I knew so well, he told me, "There are two dangers here: the jaw could be dislocated or it could be fractured." I had great confidence in him; I believed that what he was saying erred on the side of caution and told him to take another try at it. Then he went to the back of the house, into the kitchen. A few moments later, I saw him come back out with a low bench; behind him came his family, whom we also loved very much. The family did not follow him into the office. He put the bench beside the chair, picked up the forceps again and stepped up onto the bench (he was on the short side, and the added height would give him a steadier grip). After a while he gave up and one of the family members took the bench away. Never in his long career had this happened to him before. Then he took a long pointed tool and divided the molar in four; as it broke it crunched like wood being splintered by an ax. He picked up the forceps again and took out the molar as if there were four of them.

Afterwards the family came in and told me I was very brave.

That night in Mendoza, I must have abandoned our leader's face when the girls who lived in that house arrived. The poetry reciter came in too, and now she was wearing a velvet dress of a pale wine color. The bottles on the table had lost their dark color by then and their glass bodies—discreetly green—looked humiliated, like naked dowagers. When the girls came in they seemed to bring a little of the night's cool darkness with them. An agitation arose in all of us. The poetry reciter, suddenly the object of so many boys' attention, adopted a majestic stance, as if readying her entire body to be seen in accordance with some idea she had of herself. The girls greeted each other from afar and the events of the afternoon seemed to be implied in their caressing manner; one of them waved to me and used the movement of her fingers to allude to the piano. The poetry reciter, seeing the other girls greeting someone, looked at me and made a slow movement toward me with her head, as if conceding the other girls the favor of going along with their spontaneous outbursts. Some of the boys went over to the new arrivals and everything was mixed together again: the bottles gathered into groups once more but now the combinations of faces in each group were as different as dice after a new throw. Suddenly the fat girl with short hair and golden hoops in her ears came towards me. At that moment, a Chilean scout also approached, offering me a glass of wine; I began moving my hand in a way that indicated I wouldn't drink it and my fingers hit the glass: he did a juggling act with both hands to retrieve it; the glass was spilling its liquid but its rescue seemed certain. Nevertheless, in the end, it fell. While I was begging his pardon, the fat girl with the hoops was called away in another direction. My companion—the other olive-skinned one—came close to my ear and said, "The fat girl cut all her hair off because she had lice."

After a while the play of faces began to change again: they turned away, showing the backs of their necks, and accumulated in a corner of the yard. The poetry reciter had adopted the stance of one who waits for the words of a poem to assemble in her soul. It grew fairly quiet and her body was immobile. Then her lips alone began to move, and the voice that emerged was so faint it made me think of a snake charmer's flute. She kept her eyes fixed on a point in space: there she would see the poem unfurl. I realized that I could look at her with impunity and I went up as close as I could. Her face was very different from our leader's. The various parts of the poetry reciter's face didn't seem to have gathered together spontaneously: they had been placed there by the will of a person who calmly purchases the very best items from a number of shops, then joins them together in a tasteful arrangement without neglecting any detail: everything a face needed was there. In the eye shop, she had selected a large blue pair, and had carefully checked to be sure that their mechanism was perfect; no doubt she'd tried them on, swiveling them this way and that. In the mouth shop, she had chosen one of average size, but comfortable, with lips that were red and quite full. Since she was a poetry reciter, she would have taken the greatest care with this detail: she had to utter words clearly at great speed and speak slow words in veiled tones, so she had to have superior maneuverability. Indeed, her mouth was her most effective weapon. As I was observing her combined strategy—when she was raising her arms, letting her eyelids fall, and holding the words back on her lips—my eyes rested on her lips. Just when she'd almost shut off the valve of her voice entirely, her upper lip curved to one side, expressing the anguish of romantic skepticism. In the final throes of the poem, she turned her eyes towards the sky and her eyelids slowly waved their lashes like slaves fanning a rajah. During its last words, her upper lip rose and fell as deliberately as the final curtain of a show. As the edge of her lips brushed her teeth, she seemed to be tasting amorous sweet-meats, and in all of it I sensed the possibility of pleasures more subtle than the wine and empanadas on the table. Suddenly, in the middle of one of the poems, she began taking long strides to one side and the other. Since she was very tall and the strides were very long, we had to make more room for her. Instead of moving back, I took advantage of the confusion to edge forward. As she went from side to side, she didn't always turn her body and walk straight ahead; she took some sideways steps and her legs looked like a compass opening and closing. I had stopped attending to her mouth and her words. Her steps were a strange new event, not only because it was unusual to walk around like that in the middle of a poem, but also because they placed unaccustomed volumes and di-mensions into movement. Within the curving fabric of that dress, a wine-colored swell could be seen, and its ripples were slow even at the moments when the tide suddenly rose, taking those large, ro-tating volumes by surprise. On one side of the skirt was a row of buttons; the swell made them appear and disappear like the corks on a ship's rigging. It occurred to my eyes to move towards the other end of her and look at her arms, which were very white and rose higher than my head; my eyes took that expedition as if going from the sea to the clouds.

Afterwards, all of us gathered once more around the table where the wine was darker than the poetry reciter's dress and the empanadas bulged without arousing my appetite.

Not long before then I'd had to study ancient history, and though I learned very little—not enough to get me through the exam—the figures of a few goddesses and the rites of a few reli-gions remained floating in the distance. Now, looking at the poetry reciter, those floating notions drew near, bringing memories of forms and proportions that were strange to my eyes. When my eyes got bored looking down at the words and dates of history, they would escape to the illustrated pages, where they hurried across all the whiteness of the paper in pursuit of the innocent lines that formed the goddesses' bodies. Though at such moments I had forgotten them, the history book's words and dates may have participated in the feelings I was forming about that era. For despite everything, my feelings were clear, and my imagination tried to cleave through the air of that distant sky. The people and things had a strange humanity, too remote from the land of the present, but I did all I could to draw close to the life of those figures, which gave me my first encounter with extraordinary proportions and sideways steps. Now, as I watched the poetry reciter, those figures returned my visit. First they must have crossed some dark zone of my memory, then they must have sailed their stealthy ship towards the present, and finally I watched them pull away once more, taking with them a feeling of mine that was very clear—the feeling of a strange humanity. Now the poetry reciter had taken on those same proportions, embodying them with all the reality of the present moment; the white spaces within the goddesses' bodies were now filled in by this curving wine-colored dress, molding the firmness and elasticity of those curving lines. And in the poetry reciter's slow movements, not only were the lines jumbled together, violating their limits, but her innocence was also violated. It was then that I raised my eyes and they suddenly found themselves resting on the poetry reciter's white arms.

That night in Mendoza I recognized present reality by its anguish. But if I'm now tempted to say that I first became acquainted with life at nine o'clock one morning on a train, it's because that day when I left Montevideo accompanied by the Mandolión, I not only recognized that anguish once more but realized I would have it with me all my life. It would be in me even when I was thinking of the most diverse things: of the clouds that were journeying along with the train, or of the key to my house, which I carried along forgotten in my pocket without knowing when I would use it again, or of the Mandolión and the yellow ankle boot that had choked on his foot and had its tongue hanging out. But my anguish not only covered the most disparate things with its density and threw itself on any object whatsoever like a shameless woman, it also—when I was a child and my anguish was naive—used to be intermingled with strange pleasures. I remember that among all the schoolteachers of my childhood there were three who were tall and fat. Those three inspired me with the greatest respect and curiosity, but they also inspired me with a desire not to respect them. I had my secret way of disrespecting them but never put it into practice except in my imagination. The first time it occurred to me, I was living on the slope of a hill, and could enter my schoolteacher's house by walking across a plaza. She was the second of the tall, fat teachers. One morning she was walking toward the back of her house and I was following a few steps behind. I must have been about eight; she'd promised to show me a hen with chicks. As soon as we arrived, the hen began clucking and from under her black-and-white spotted body peeked some tiny yellow chicks. It must have been nice and warm under there. The schoolteacher had on a skirt of a gray color very similar to the hen's. And at home that day, after lunch, when they forced me to take a siesta, I began imagining to myself how lovely it would be to live underneath the teacher's skirt. It must be nice and warm there, too, and her legs, above the stockings, must be very white. In my daydream I imagined that it would all seem very natural to the teacher: while I was beneath her skirt she would gaze distractedly off in another direction, and if I touched one of her legs she would be as still and calm as the hen with her chicks.

In those days I didn't aspire to make older people take all my desires into account. They'd already given me an idea of their customs, and when I saw that an impulse of mine went beyond what was permitted, I silenced it and tried to bring it off covertly, and finally resigned myself to imagining that I was fulfilling it. Thus the adults would go their way and I would go mine and we would all be at peace. Of course before resigning myself, I would try every possible means of carrying out my impulse; I chose the siesta hour for those experiments because the daylight frightened me and because at that hour the adults had their eyes closed. But if I were to put myself beneath a woman's skirts she would have to be standing up, in which case she would no longer be having a siesta. So I had to resign myself to trying it out on a woman who was awake. One summer night my whole family was enjoying the cool air along the sidewalk. I'm not sure exactly when my aunt got up from her chair and took it inside. But I remember the moment when her big white skirt startled me, moving across the dark courtyard. She was setting the table, and made many trips back and forth to the kitchen. A large lamp hanging from the ceiling of the dining room cast light over the tablecloth; but I stuck my head out from under the table— where I had crawled—and turning it to one side, almost resting it on the floor, I peered up inside her skirt. Everything was very dark. It only grew a little lighter when, to reach a dish on the other side of the table, she rested her weight on one foot and lifted the other into the air. I repeated the operation several times without letting my head touch her feet. After clearing off the table, she came back one last time, but with slow steps; I thought she'd seen me. She approached the edge of the table again and stood still for a moment; I didn't know what she might be doing. A sound of crickets filled my head; she sat down at the table, lifting one foot and leaving the other on the ground. With great caution, I stuck out my head— this time outside the skirt—and, looking up, discovered that her face was concealed behind a book. I was on very good terms with my aunt. Crawling under her skirt might be no more than a joke. I decided to go in slowly but as soon as she felt me she let out a great scream; I went scurrying to my bed and those out on the sidewalk ran to the dining room. It gave my aunt a kind of attack. There was a police station across from my house and they sent a policeman over to ask what had happened. At home they said that the commissioner had some feelings for my aunt.

My failure didn't upset me; after the world had answered my desire with such violence and I'd had such a fright I was glad that the consequences hadn't been even worse and that they'd said nothing to me at home that evening or the next day. What was more: that night I thought I heard laughter.

But in Mendoza, when I was more than fourteen, I had once again encountered the anguish left in me by things that were impossible. It isn't that I aspired to carry out a definitive experiment such as dwelling beneath a skirt like an explorer living in a tent. That night in Mendoza, I'd primed myself to attempt a covert task: I would approach the circle of admirers surging around the poetry reciter and the moment she ran her eyes over the area where I was standing, I would take advantage of the opportunity to place a few words of praise within her reach. She might stumble against my words and, for a minute, mingle her soul with mine. I would be trembling, but I had to find it within me to size up her will and evoke some feeling of sympathy. I was certain of being very experienced in love, and it didn't matter that, for the moment, I was unacquainted with the moment when lovers need to be alone. I knew the feelings that bring them to the verge of solitude—that was the main thing; the rest might happen at any moment. Given the few days we would be spending in Mendoza, a violent offensive might have been expedient, but such a thing was not in keeping with my dignity, and moreover any suggestion of a struggle between two people of such different volumes—she was three times more corpulent than I was—would have gone down badly. Furthermore, I couldn't give up the pleasure of entering a woman's soul slowly and making myself at home inside her, with my piano and my books. In any case, I decided to move towards the poetry reciter's orbit; going over the words I would speak to her, I waited for the moment when her gaze would fall on me. As soon as she saw me she lowered her eyebrows, as if to hide her gaze behind them. She had no choice but to hear out my words. I was stringing them together at the slow pace I would need to carry heavy stones to where they would form the foundation of a very solid house, many stories high. She prepared herself to begin lowering her eyelids, and she had started to heave a sigh that was swelling her out in a very impressive way, when a girl begged my pardon and said something to a boy from Mendoza who was beside me. He was a short, fat boy whose hair stood straight up and he, too, had prepared himself to listen to me; he was poised as if intent on doing whatever he could to help me get the words off my chest. Immediately after the interruption, I started to say everything again. As I was speaking, I thought the others would notice I was using the same words and realize that this was a speech I'd rehearsed in advance, but I couldn't hold back my explanations about ancient history and the poetry reciter's strides. She couldn't contain herself either and interrupted me, saying that she strode about like that because unlike most reciters of poetry she had "staging." Then she spoke of the future of poetry recitation and of what they were paying in the Buenos Aires theaters. When I finally managed to remove myself from her circle, I felt like an empty room—even I wasn't inside it. A moment earlier, the poetry reciter had tried to change my ideas and rearrange the things in my room her own way; but her sideways strides, in the interpretation she gave them, struck me as nonsensical gimmickry, and having the idea of what they were paying in Buenos Aires continually in mind was like wanting to make my room into a house of commerce. Though I would never allow her to rearrange my room, for a few moments I felt as though I had lost touch with my own inner world; now my room was arranged by no one, neither me nor her, and the thing that least belonged there was the idea of love.

The irritation that had beset me as I left the reciter's circle made me wander for a while among the groups around the table. I walked around with my room in a mess and no inclination to put it in order.

After some time had gone by—enough time for the dust that had been stirred up in my room to settle—I felt that my legs were heavy. I was enduring my anguish as if it were a woman who had chosen me from among many others before I was ever born: the more depressed she saw I was, the more she threw herself at me. And worst of all, I was feeling rather complacent about this. I needed to abandon myself to thinking about my own anguish.

Suddenly it occurred to me to look for a chair. My body, which had been coming to pester me with its weariness for some time, had brought up this idea. I also thought of the dialogue I might have with my anguish if I could ignore the body; if I sat it down in a chair, it would busy itself digesting the empanadas and the wine and would leave me and my anguish in peace. But at the last moment the body held back. Of course it didn't tell me so openly, but began with some halfhearted but astute work in my thoughts, and finally came out with the notion that everyone else there was standing up and it would look bad if I were to sit down. When I desisted from going to look for a chair, it heaved a great sigh. But after that it didn't make the lungs do much work. The intervals between breaths grew longer and longer. My anguish was slowly moving to fill up an unknown space within me. I was no longer an empty room, now I was a dark cave on whose floor, strewn with wet straw, a boa, just awakening from its lethargy, moved about in the warm, sticky atmosphere. Miasmas rose to my head and ended up as words. But those words—which seemed to have passed through many mouths to reach me in different voices that must have come across unfamiliar times and places—now presented themselves to demand a significance I had never granted them. Not long before they arrived in my head I had, through my darkness, divined their imminence. These words had been trailing me for a while, and now, in that gathering, had waited for the moment to find me alone

and, taking advantage of my disillusionment with the poetry reciter, had drawn near to start making their prophetic intentions re-
sound within me, just when I was feeling most anguished. Though
the voices were as faded as garments left out in bad weather, their
meaning was expressed with all the confidence that would be con-
veyed by a mouth that speaks for this world while its eyes are fixed
on another.

I had already listened to these and other words on many occasions. But they weren't always addressed to me. Sometimes my
head was like a ramshackle tavern in the middle of a fair; all sorts
of words came in while I stared out the window. And I listened to
many words that weren't addressed to me. As they came in, they
went by me and I didn't pay much attention to them. Some just
came to pass the time or for the pure pleasure of chatting. Others,
when their physiognomies could be made out through the haze of
cigarette smoke, seemed to be there on fishy business.

This was the tavern where the words that had been trailing me
suddenly arrived. They were only just starting to gather when I
realized they'd been formulating a judgment and were about to give
me some advice. The first ones were like recent arrivals, taking their
places around a large table. Then, when the circle was closed, they
put their conclusion on the table. It referred, no doubt, to what had
happened to me a few moments before with the poetry reciter. This
is what it said: "If you wish to cross the world with another person
on your arm, you will have to hear her out to the end." I paid more
attention to the conclusion than to the physiognomy of the words
that brought it. Nevertheless, by some accident, three of the words
were "on your arm." At first, when those words entered my tavern,
I didn't much notice them. "Arm" was the important word and "on
your" was like a little dog following behind it. While all that was
happening, my body had remained in the middle of that courtyard,
breathing at long intervals, just as I'd left it. And suddenly several
boys—who were running to see something, I didn't know what—

carried it off with them. And one of the boys said, "at least he had two girls *on his arm*." I barely had time to recognize the little dog trailing the important word, now outside my tavern. I experienced the abrupt change as if I'd suddenly fallen to the ground and found my hands clawing at the earth. Then it turned out that the boys who'd carried off my body were running towards a spot in the courtyard where there was a brick-lined pit that must have been half a meter deep. There, in a moment of distraction, our leader had put half his leg. And the boys helped him out. Afterwards he gave his smile and rubbed his hands together, and I recognized his innocence. Then, offering his arms to the girls again, he went strolling off with them. He took great pleasure in that stroll. I wondered if he would take the same pleasure in strolling with two old women as with two girls. Answering this question was somewhat complicated for me, and feeling reluctant to do so, I left it aside for later. In any case, his emotions were freer than the poetry reciter's. He could allow his feelings to spill out over anything, the first thing he found before his eyes.

When I first joined the "Vanguards" and he was teaching us the organization's rules and regulations, he had spent a lot of time explaining that a Vanguard should give service and expect nothing in return. He gave many examples of this, but one in particular stayed in my memory: whenever we found a banana peel on the sidewalk we were to toss it into the street so that no one else would slip on it as they walked by. I was curious about what would happen when a banana peel was tossed into the street without expecting anything in return. My first encounter with a banana peel happened when I was out walking with my parents one night, accompanied by a distant cousin, already well along in years, of whom they spoke disapprovingly. I saw the peel several yards away and walked a few paces ahead to pick it up by its short stem: it was deep yellow and its inner lining was fairly white. After I had tossed it, the distant cousin said, "Why did you do that?"

"So that somebody else doesn't step on it and slip."

"You're kidding. What do you care about somebody else?"

My parents and I remained silent. Then they spoke about other things. At first this irritated me. Then I was carried, as if by a wave pushing me gently along, towards the memory of people and places where I was continually hearing things like that said. More and more of these people crowded into the memory, bringing me a certain feeling of reality or common sense in which my new conduct appeared strange and affected. If those people and that distant cousin had known what our leader told us they would have made fun of it. But that feeling lasted only a few moments, because immediately I found my footing once more and again felt the happiness of belonging to a secret band whose signal was tossing banana peels into the street. Another time that I encountered a banana peel I was wearing my Vanguard uniform. The sun was very bright and it was the silent hour of the siesta. I was going along the only stretch of Calle Asención that hadn't been subdivided into blocks. A white sidewalk ran along the edge of a vast alfalfa field and from afar I saw the yellow banana peel in the middle of the sidewalk. That day, the idea of the banana peel as a harmful thing was far from my thoughts; it was thoroughly likable with its bright yellow color, and what was more it lent itself to the ritual of my secret band. I don't know why, but instead of throwing it into the street I had the idea of throwing it into the alfalfa field; I readied my arm so that the peel would go far, but then, when I saw the small yellow spot fall and disappear so abruptly into that immensity of green, it made me a little sad. I looked at the green of the alfalfa, rippling in the breeze, and felt a certain sorrow at the thought that the small banana peel which had been in my hands an instant earlier and had been a little bit mine, had, at my hand, met with the destiny of being swallowed up by that immense field. But at that point it would have been very difficult to jump over the barbed-wire fence and look for it among all that alfalfa.

I was rather surprised to encounter these memories, and thought that perhaps they might have been aroused by the other banana peel that was now in front of me as I was travelling on the train accompanied by the Mandolión, who had pushed it under the seat with his yellow boot.

But back then, on that night in Mendoza, I had yet another surprise. It happened as I was thinking of the pleasure that our leader must feel walking with two girls on his arms, when I heard some talk behind me about roast cat. After a few moments, I'd turned around very discreetly, though I had no great desire to know who was emitting exclamations of astonishment because such an animal had been cooked. It turned out to be the wife of the Mendoza leader. From their conversation, it appeared that the other woman was the daughter of a man who ran a charcuterie. Some time before, an old Indian had been hired to work in the charcuterie, and it was he who had showed them how to roast a cat. The daughter of the sausage maker was explaining the form the sacrifice must take, and when she reached the point where the cat, skinned and split open, had to be seasoned and left outside overnight before being cooked, I couldn't help imagining the skinned body, its head—not only still covered in fur but also with its whiskers still on—making a grimace that revealed both rows of teeth. It was while I was imagining this that I received the surprise: suddenly I realized that the voice behind me was known to me. I spun around and found myself looking at the poetry reciter.

At first it felt as if my eyes had been emptied out—and she was beginning to fill them up again. My idea of the poetry reciter gave a great lurch, and for a few minutes I lost all sense of her person and stumbled about aimlessly. I barely felt it when the trace of illusion that had somehow remained hidden inside me vanished; the surprise forced me to form another idea of her immediately. The simple fact of the charcuterie unveiled other facts that were implicated in it. She was thinking about what they were paying in

Buenos Aires, and about the future of poetry recitation and her rivalry with those who "had no staging." All of that must have been pondered in a shop that sold sausages and cold cuts. I was starting to get angry, as if I'd been swindled. I had discovered that beneath the poetry reciter lay a sausage maker. She had no right to arouse illusions as a poetry reciter, or to fill up my eyes, like someone stuffing a sausage, with her body that was so large and, at that moment, so close. I thought of the words "sausage maker" with derision and ignoble joy, in revenge for my amorous failure—but by that very night, not long before I fell asleep, I had already reconciled the idea of sausage maker with that of poetry reciter and felt more inclined to allow myself a little sadness.

They had made up a lone bed for me in a small room where a dressmaker's dummy stood. I had put out the light, but more came in from the courtyard through the shutters' slats to shine on the great pink bust of the dummy which, in place of a head, was topped with a black knob. I turned my face to the wall. Despite my weariness, I couldn't sleep and began imagining the poetry reciter in her sausage shop, wrapping up a thick, pale slab of lard. As she did up the packet, she was chatting, and then suddenly while one hand was holding the paper, the other was spinning its white plumpness through the air at the same time as the mouth was saying, "I'll send it over to you later." I remembered the pirouettes those very hands had made while she was reciting. Just as I was about to think that those movements were ridiculous, I was interrupted by the idea that the poetry reciter was the daughter of foreigners, perhaps from some country that lay in the north of the world. Then I thought that they must have brought those hand movements from there, wrapped up in other customs. But still, a moment before I went to sleep, I pictured the poetry reciter sitting in a swing, one hand gripping the rope as the other made the same pirouette I had seen while she was reciting, but this time the little twist served to indicate to the public that the demonstration was over.

My sleep seemed to be tranquilly doing its work that night. But suddenly I woke up with a cry of terror. I found myself sitting up in bed. And even after I was awake I could still see the three doors; they stood in a place where there were three streets, and each door opened onto one of the streets. I saw them from the outside, closed, and, inexplicably, I saw them all at once. When I awoke, I immediately had a sense of the house I found myself in, but I didn't know the position of my bed in relation to the rest of the room. Then I remembered the dummy, but I couldn't locate it either. My throat was a little raw from the scream, but I didn't wonder why I'd been terrified by things as innocent as those three doors; at other times, in other dreams, the same thing had happened. Before abandoning myself to thinking about the doors again, I wanted to know where my bed was in relation to the dummy. When I was lying in the dark, it was always difficult for me to extend a hand out of bed because I thought that if my hand were to encounter another hand that wasn't mine I would go mad. Nevertheless, reaching out my left hand I touched the wall and quickly realized that the dummy stood at my feet and the door lay in the same direction. I already had a certain feeling for that bed; I'd decided it was a good one because it had allowed me to lie on it and had stood still and kept something of my warmth while giving me a little of its own. The dummy inspired me with a certain feeling of mistrust: as soon as I grew distracted its bust suggested the presence of another person, and its head—the size of a knob— seemed to give it petty ideas. But my strongest feeling that night was produced by the three doors in my dream. I buried my whole body back in the bed.

My eyes, now freed from the task of remembering the positions of the objects in that room, went off to the place in the dream where the three doors were and I began to relive—but awake, this time—the feeling I'd had when I was asleep. It was as if my wakeful curiosity had been left outside a house made of glass. I'd told it

that when I was about to fall asleep or something unpleasant was
about to happen to me it should break the glass and wake me up
completely. And in that way I went back into the still warm region
of my dream and found the same strange sense of purpose and terrifying meaning. Once again I tasted that decoction of the soul,
and the atmosphere charged with malevolent silence exhaled by
the three doors. Even so I didn't relive the events of the dream for
very long. The wide awake persona of mine who was waiting outside the glass house called to me in alarm; I went out to it, abandoning the region of the dream. And when I learned what it had
discovered my scalp tingled once more. Until then I had thought it
was the dream that cast an evil shadow over those three innocent
doors. But my persona who was keeping watch had a sudden, anguished memory and recognized the dream's three doors. A while
before, I'd been told that a certain charcuterie in Europe was famous for its pork products. The manufacturer's secret was to mix
human flesh and blood in with the pork. The victims were re-
cruited from among the shop's clientele at the busiest hour of the
day. Some who went in were invited to step into the back, on the
pretext of being shown some new product, and never came out
again. When questioned about it, the shop's owners talked about
the large crowd of customers and some possible mix-up, and said
they didn't know which of the shop's three doors the person might
have exited through. But once a chambermaid's boyfriend was
waiting in front of one of the doors for her to come out; that was
where they usually met up. When she didn't appear after a long
time, the boyfriend went to the police in alarm, and thus the truth
was learned. When I was told the story, I'd had to imagine three
doors opening onto three streets, and now they had come back in
my dream. But though they had appeared without their story, I
had felt as much terror as if the story had been present; the story
may have been hiding behind the closed doors, making a display of
indifference. Perhaps if I'd been able to open them and see what

was behind I wouldn't have found the story; it could have remained submerged in the surfaces of the doors, saturating them with a curse that would harm anyone who looked at them; they would taint the depths of his eyes with a poison that could never be erased.

It didn't strike me as strange that my dreams brought me a charcuterie after what had happened with the poetry reciter; I already knew that they liked to compose their ravings out of a subject close at hand. But the fact that the sausage shop had been hidden, and I'd had to discover it after I woke up and excavated in my memory, made me shiver. I was even more startled when I remembered that my scalp had tingled an instant before my discovery of the story and how it coincided with the poetry reciter's charcuterie.

After I had let out the scream that made the walls of my dream collapse and left me with my eyes wide open in the middle of the night, I kept sifting through the rubble to see where the scream had come from. When I thought of who it might have been, my scalp tingled once more: it might have been the cat. The idea I had formed of its death, with its grimace and its cry, could have been just as present and hidden as the crimes of the sausage makers. The cat's soul, abandoning its body, exhaled with its final cry, must have gone on navigating within that sound like a soul in purgatory. And that night, finding a sympathetic instrument in my body, it had vibrated once more.

All at once I realized that I had thrown off all my terror and was left with a clean spirit. I let my head go on thinking useless thoughts like a father allowing his child to stir water with a little stick. After much wandering, my thoughts reassembled around the poetry reciter. By now my curiosity about her was quite lethargic; I knew it would be impossible for me to understand her, but I paused to contemplate my memory of her once more, as if I were spending a moment leafing through the book I had closest

to hand. While the influence of the dream lasted, I had felt hostility mixed with fear towards her, but now I thought of her simply as a person who was strange. From what I had learned, she
struck me as capable of sincere sacrifice; she could have sacrificed
the cat to a god she loved with all her soul, but she would also be
capable of getting up in the middle of the night and saying to
herself, "The sacrifice of the cat to God was sincere, but sym-
bolic; in reality, God has no interest in eating the cat." And then
she would have eaten it.

The next day I started to get up before they called me; that
way I could get dressed slowly and allow my eyes to wander about
in no great hurry, looking at one thing and another. Nevertheless
I noticed that while I was distracted my eyes had touched on the
bust of the dummy and instantly withdrew their gaze. I had
taught them never to linger over a woman's bust, and now, in-
stinctively, they were proceeding as if they were seeing a real
bust. Then, in another moment of distraction while I was but-
toning my clothes, I happened to be standing next to the dummy,
and its insistent allusion to a flesh-and-blood person again dis-
turbed me. Then the thought that every room of that house must
have an object in it that defended the room by its mere presence
forced me to be cautious.

Suddenly I stopped remembering what had happened inside
that house and instead went back to feeling, with some of the sensations of the first time, the surprise of the streets and the air and
the sky of Mendoza above the trees and the houses. But before I
went back to sleeping in my memories, like someone who wakes up
for a moment while his body is turning over, I saw—during the
journey a train was making ten years later—that the seat opposite
me was empty and, consulting my eyes' memory, I deduced that
the Mandolión had been gone for a while, which was how I'd had
such a long stretch of remembering. I got up to take some note-

books I had written on that trip to Chile out of my bag, since I didn't remember if certain things in Mendoza had happened on the outward or the return journey. As I was rummaging through my bag, someone opened the door of the car and I saw the Mandolión sipping *mate* in the second-class coach.

I decided to submerge myself in my notebooks; I would review them with all the painstaking care a doctor would employ in examining a man about to get married. The night before, thinking that when I left Montevideo I would have to change my life, I had decided to first investigate my earlier life, which was why I was carrying my whole written history in a corner of my bag.

I had two notebooks from the trip to Chile; one was small and contained a concise daily account of events, just as our leader had ordained; after the journey, someone in our organization had had it bound in a cover of "a serious color," I believe it was sepia. The other notebook was large, intimate, written at random intervals and full of inexplicable stupidities. Its binding was the color of tobacco, and very greasy.

On my first morning in Mendoza, many things had the audacity to be different from the things in my country, but so innocently that I was enchanted and went running to note them down in the intimate notebook. A companion of ours appeared in it, raising one hand almost to the level of his shoulder and saying, "Last winter the snow came up to here." I had to quickly imagine a winter with snow; I had no recollection at hand in my memory to help me. Nevertheless, a snowy winter quickly appeared, pieced together out of who knows what residue of imagery. But what took the greatest effort was imagining it there, on that bright, gravelly street with sunlight and trees like the trees in my own country. Also, whenever I'd looked at figures standing in snow, my soul had always grown as grave and quiet as a silent movie. Now this young boy who had lived through a snowy winter remained very cheerful, much like someone who had never seen snow. So I had no alternative but to think something new about snowy winters. And to top it all off, the boy had said, ". . . the snow came up to here."

Note:

Only a fragment of "Lands of Memory" was published during Felisberto's lifetime, in a Montevideo magazine called *La Plata* in June of 1944. The novel was first published in its entirety by Ediciones Arca in 1965, a year after his death.